AFRICA SPEAKS

AFRICA SPEAKS

BY

MARK GOLDBLATT

THE PERMANENT PRESS
SAG HARBOR, NY 11963

Library of Congress Cataloging-in-Publication Data

Goldblatt, Mark
    Africa Speaks /by Mark Goldblatt
      p. cm.
    ISBN 1-57962-037-X (alk paper)
    1. African American men--Fiction. 2. New York (NY)--Fiction.
    3. Young men--Fiction. 4. Gangs--Fiction. I. Title

PS3607.O45 A69 2002
813'.6--dc21   200103036616
                                                            CIP

Manufactured in the United States.

THE PERMANENT PRESS
4170 Noyac Road
Sag Harbor, NY 11963

"We the target. If you go over to the top of the totem pole of life: which is white man/ white woman, Asian man/ Asian woman, Mexican man/ Mexican woman. Then the fuckin' funny shit is then it's Black woman/ Black Nigga. The Nigga'z at the bottom. They give everybody a job except a Nigga. We are the most threatening because we genetically can create everybody. What Western Civilization has done is went throughout the whole world and taught everybody else how to look down on us, how to disrespect us . . . So that dynamic is everywhere and my whole point is that we are the target and we gonna get fucked over . . . cause this system wasn't made for the Nigga. . . . I'm Creole: my grandmother speaks French. I happen to be dark. If I came out light maybe I'd feel different because I would somehow fit in. I just happen to have the hair and a pointy nose and some chinky eyes. But I'm Black as fuck so I gotta live with this everyday, and maybe that makes me more aware. . . My whole point at the end of the day is AmeriKKKa was made by white men for white men. . . . This shit is made for rich elite, by the rich elite. So they can exploit the fuck outta y'all and me. So until we get man enough and educated enough to say, Let's just break this shit off, we ain't shit!"

—Ras Kass

"I have a dream."

—Martin Luther King

Now?

A *salaam aleichem,* in the name of Allah, the merciful, the compassionate, the one true God. *Yo, yo, yo,* I'd like to send a shout out to my people, to my kings and queens. You know what I'm saying? *My kings and queens.* Yo, and a special shout out to my soldiers, my niggas in arms, the One-Forty-Ninth Street Crew—vagina findas, *no doubt.* Crazy mad dawgs! I got nothing but love for you. Even you, Herc! It's all good. The name's Africa Ali, I'm just 23, and I'm about to drop the four-one-one. Just keeping it real, 'cause that's what I'm all about. Reality to the *utmost.* But first I got one last holler. To my brother Biggie. Notorious B.I.G. He kept it real.

Is that thing on?

Now don't go getting that look on your face. I ain't avoiding your question. I ain't the type to bail neither just 'cause I finished my egg roll. *Did Tawana tell the truth?* That's what you want to know, right? Well, it's deep. It's like the sixty-nine dollar question. So don't rush me. I'm working it around inside my brain. Now, then, I've got the answer. The answer to the sixty-nine dollar question. It's yes and no. That's it, that's the answer. Now let me break it down for you: I ain't saying Tawana told *the* truth. What I'm saying is she told *a* truth. You know what I'm saying? What I mean is black folks been fucked over and shit on by the white man the last five hundred years. So whether or not one particular white man, Pagano, or whatever his name was, whether Pagano fucked over and shit on one particular black girl, Tawana, what difference it makes? It's what's called a *mood* point. The truth depends on what kind of mood you're in.

Now, I see you smiling. You're not used to a black man speaking his mind, am I right? You see a black man, and you think, "There goes a baller" or "There goes a banger." But you don't think, "There goes an intellectual." So I see you're watching me, right now, out the corner of your eye, and I know you're wondering which is it going to be, the baller or the banger? Except now you're upset, you're smiling 'cause you don't know what else to do, you're like in turmoil, 'cause I don't fit into your stereotypes.

But that's the power of the black man. He can look you in the eye, and just like *snap* he can look right through you. Right down to your soul. It's an African thing; it's a connection to the spiritual side. It's like our ancestors, they're still alive inside us. Did you know the Nubians could levitate themselves? It's a well-known fact. Just float on up into the sky and chill. But when I say chill, I mean like *chill*. No heartbeat. No breathing. Nothing. You know what I'm saying? It's like you'd get a dozen of 'em just hanging out, up a hundred feet in the air, just chilling, dead to the world. It was a glory to behold! The white man ever do that? Hell no! 'Cause the white man, he never had it. That connection to the spirit, to the sky.

The truth is, I feel kind of sorry for the white man. Really, I do. I'm not one of these brothers who rolls out of bed in the morning and thinks to himself, "Let's see . . . what can I do to scare whitey today?" You know the type. It's in the way they cross the street, like as if to say *fuck you* with how they're crossing against the red light. Nothing but fools if you ask me. Like stepping in front of a yellow cab is going to make up for five hundred years of living in chains. But yet I'll tell you what. It works. That cabbie, he ain't going to honk at no nigga. Not unless he's a towel and doesn't know no better. But even towels . . . what? Towels. You know, *towelheads*—Arabs. Towelheads. Even they learn. You can honk a chink, you can honk a Jew. You can even honk a spic if he's by himself. But a nigga, well, that's another story. You don't go honking no nigga! 'Cause he be *crazy.* You know what I'm saying? He might just haul you right out of that driver's seat, might just knock you on your towel-wearin' goat-bonin' ass.

Herc's like that. He's my blood, don't get me wrong, but it's like he just goes crazy insane if he gets disrespected. No use talking to him; he gets that look in his eyes and he's gone. Crazy insane motherfucker. That's Herc. It's not his real name. His real name is Khallid. I always kind of liked that name. It fits him. But then he started to work out. You know, pump. Wound up with mad pecs. Pure cock diesel. You know what I'm saying? So the homeboys, they started calling him Herc. Short for Hercules. He took to it too. That's how it became his street name.

So me and Herc, we walking home from court last week. You know, *court*—hoops is what I mean. We were walking up Sixth Avenue, probably between 22nd and 23rd Streets, and walking toward us is a suit. Little white guy, maybe five-foot-six, no hair, no chin. The thing is, he's so busy just gabbing away on his cell phone, he don't even notice us. He's just gabbing and gabbing. He's going to walk right into the two of us—me and Herc. Now me, I just step out of his way. I mean, what's the point? You know? But Herc, he knocks the guy right on his bony white ass. Just drops his shoulder, and then *boom;* next thing you know, the guy's sprawled out on the sidewalk. Cell phone's cracked wide open, batteries rolling down Sixth Avenue. Briefcase lying in the gutter, papers blowing every which way. Then Herc leans down and gets right in the guy's face, and then he screams, *"Yo!"*

What he means is, *What you gonna do about it?*

So the guy just slides backwards on his butt, like as if he's a crab, sliding out of Herc's way, and then me and Herc just move on. We go another couple of blocks, not saying a word about what happened. Then I turn to Herc, and I'm like, "Why you go and do that for, Herc? What that little white man ever do to you?"

Then Herc says, "1555—that's how I'm living!"

That's when I knew he was right. Wrong in a way, but right in a bigger way. You know what I'm saying? That white man gabbing away on that cell phone—you go back a hundred years, and it ain't stocks and bonds he's buying and selling. No, it's niggas.

It's hard to explain that kind of shit to white folks. It's like a *concept,* yo, like no matter how much it's explained to them, they just don't get it. 'Cause they ain't never been in that situation. Like I said, I don't wake up in the morning looking to scare the white man. But I go down to the subway station, and I read that sign that says *NO SPIT- TING,* and I just want to spit. Even if I'm bone dry, even if I never would've thought of spitting, the second I see that sign *NO SPITTING* . . . it's like the one thing in the world I want to do. It's funny in a way, kind of; it's like the sign's saying to me, "Go on, nigga, I dare you!"

It's like a dis.

You know what *dis* means, don't you? Dis, like in *disre- spect.* All right, I just thought I'd ask. I like to be compre- hended—you know what I'm saying? Comprehension to the *utmost.* I talk to white people sometimes, and you'd think I was talking chink to them. They get this screwed up look on their faces like *Huh?* Or what's that white saying . . . *Come again?* Like I was a ho, and they just did me a favor going down on me.

That's another thing I've noticed about white people. Well, white women at least. Naturally, I can't say if it's true for white men. But white women—even when they go down on you, they don't *go down.* What I mean is, like, they're down there, they're getting busy, but it's like they're not down there. They're somewhere else. I waxed this one bitch called Nancy. Straight up boo-yaa. Nice titties, the kind that fill up your hands but don't spill out. Just out of high school. Maybe five-six, five-seven. Blond too—and when I say blond, I mean curtains *and* carpet. So the two of us, we're out back of her folks' house, we're getting busy, we're rolling around on the grass, and then she's going down on me, and she's bobbin' and jobbin'. But then I suddenly realize, it ain't me. No, it's the Black Man. Like with capital letters. She was doing me, no doubt, but yet at the same time she was doing the *idea* of doing a black man.

So I grabbed her by the hair, and I dragged her up, and I said to her, "Who you doing, Nancy? Me or Malcolm?"

Then she's like, "Malcolm who?"

"Malcolm *who?*" I said.

Then she said, "I thought your friend's name was Jerome."

"I'm talking Malcolm *X!*"

"But he's dead," she said.

She didn't get it. She didn't *comprehend.* Didn't under-dig. Dig? So I rolled on out of there. Well, first I let her finish me off. Right afterwards, though, I was like, *See ya, wouldn't want to be ya.*

Nothing against Malcolm—he's my man. *By any means necessary.* I mean, *damn,* the brother could bring it! *By any means necessary.* Word! That says it all. Now Jesse, he's wack. It's like the one thing me and my old man ever agreed on . . . the fact that Jesse's wack. Him and his wack *Rainbow Coalition.* You ain't no rainbow, negro! You a *black man.* Be proud, nigga! Your ancestors were *gods.* Word up! The white man, he thinks he's all that 'cause he flies to the moon. But a thousand years ago, the black man was already flying across the damn universe. It would be like Wednesday, and he'd think, "Well, it's Wednesday—time to ride out to Alpha Uranus." Shit like that. But he didn't make no big deal about it. He just hopped into his rocket and took off. Back the next day too—

My old man?

He teaches history at Francis Lewis High School. We don't talk too much no more. But I remember he used to call Jesse *the Fortune Cookie Man.* Said that was what he sounded like—damn fortune cookie. Plus, now, whenever I hear Jesse on the news, he's like *people-of-color* this and *people-of-color* that. People of color? Yo, I got news for you, bitch! You *one* color! Greatest damn color in the world.

You ain't no yellow chink. You ain't no beenie-wearin' Jew. You ain't no spic-talking spic.

Stop fronting, nigga!

Now the chinks, they *love* Jesse. They're always out there, right up front, at his marches, and they're like: "Yes, we people of color! We chinky yellow! Yellow color! We just like you!" But I'm like: *Yo, when was your children ever sold down the river?* I hear chinks saying that, *people of color,* I just want to wet their chinky asses. They're just looking to piggyback the situation of black folks. Chink bitches especially. Of course, it don't surprise me—being that chink men got yellow pencil dicks. And when I say pencil dicks, I don't mean no straight up number twos neither. I mean the kind that's sharpened down till it's almost not there. Jew boys ain't much bigger. Then the rab comes along, and he snips off another inch. Word! Who says Jews so smart? That rab, he shows up, and he's like *snip.* What does he do? Collect 'em in jars?

I waxed a chink once—I mean, you got to do *one.* Now, let me explain what it's like. Waxing a chink is like wearing butter underwear. Ain't nothing on God's green earth smoother than chink pussy. I think that's what heaven must be like, you know, smooth and snug. The best thing is, you don't even have to work the bitch. After she's twatted so many pencil dicks, it's like suddenly she's got hold of a damn black nightstick. So here's how you fuck a chink. You just lie on your back and let her do the fucking. Maybe you can catch a little tube, or maybe call out for pizza; it don't matter to her 'cause she's got a *man* inside her. You know what I'm saying? I spell M-A-N!

Straight up, I boned about every kind of bitch there is. Black, white, yellow, what have you. 'Ricans too. Lots of 'Ricans. *Hola boriqua*—represent! Young. Old. Hundreds of 'em—I lost count around ninety. I ain't even counting chickenheads. Blow-jobs, I mean. Number one playa from the Himalaya. But I'd say most of the females I been with were black. For one thing, they give it up quickest. They got to 'cause it's the one thing they got over white bitches. Ain't no black female as fine as a fine white bitch—I ain't afraid to say it neither. Yo, that's the reason, check it out, you didn't never see no white dancer in a Salt 'N Pepa video. It's 'cause the director, he knew if you put a white dancer in the shot, ain't no one going to pay no attention to Salt 'N Pepa. That's the first thing dead presidents get you—Caucasian pussy. That's just the way it is. It ain't fair. I ain't proud of it. I wish our females were as fine as white bitches. But they ain't. So they got to give it up.

Like I was saying, I been with every kind of bitch there is. I got one kid in 201 I know about for sure, and I got a ho in 718 telling me I got another kid in the oven. I doubt it though 'cause she's a hoodrat. Been dug out more often than the damn Panama Canal. So who knows—

What? You don't think I'm a good father?

How can I be a father when the skank ho won't let me near the brat? Look, I was there when he got born; I wanted to call him Africa Jr., but then the bitch went and called him DeWayne. *DeWayne!* What kind of negro name is that? I'd rather name the kid *Two*—you know, short for 201.

You ever seen a baby get born?

Yo, that shit is *nasty!* Once you see that motherfucker come squirting out, *word,* you never want to go down there again. You know what I'm saying? It's like, one second you got a ho cake, the next second you got like a garbage chute! But I rode the rail out to Jersey City just to be there, just to watch the brat get born. So Tanya's got her feet up in the metal things, and I'm right there next to her, and she's puffing and puffing, and I'm whispering, "Just breathe, Tanya. That's it, baby. You're doing real good."

Then suddenly she's like, "Tell me you love me, Kevin."

That's my slave name—Kevin.

So, anyway, she's like, "Tell me you love me."

I kind of duck the question and say, "It's all good, Tanya."

But she's still saying, "Tell me you love me, Kevin."

Now I ain't going to lie to the bitch. So I kind of change the subject, and I say to her, "Just breathe, baby."

But she won't let it go. "Tell me you love me, Kevin. Say the words."

"What difference it makes if I say the words, Tee?"

"Just say them."

"It's just words."

Then for no reason she's like, "Get out! Get out! Get out!" She's cussing at me, calling me a motherfucker. After I got on the train and rode to fucking Jersey! I was about to roll on out too, but then it happened. The brat came sliding out of her, and the doc—he cleaned him off and handed him to me. And I'm like *damn!* You know what I'm talking about? *Damn!*

That was the last time Tanya ever let me hold him. Soon as I handed him over to the bitch, she told me to take a hike.

Yo, I didn't let the door hit me on the way out neither!

That's what you white boys don't seem to comprehend: *Women ain't men.* You deal with a woman like you're dealing with a man, you turn her into a dyke. They got it in them anyway—the taste for pussy. So it just takes a little nudge, you know, and they're diving for tuna. You got to treat a bitch like she's a bitch. Now I see white boys like yourself, they're out walking with their bitches, talking to 'em, listening to 'em like they got something to say. Fronting is what I'm saying. But here's what I'm about: *If you got to front, it ain't worth it.* Pussy is pussy. It's out there, miles of it, from sea to shining sea. If you miss a piece, so be it. You catch the next one.

So white boys ask me, "Hey, Africa, how come you catch so much pussy?"

Now here comes the answer: 'Cause I don't front for it!

It's just business with me—pussy, I mean. It's like a *commodity.* Not just pussy though. I'm talking everything is a commodity. Face is a commodity. Pussy. What have you.

It's all commodities. The thing is, black women don't got the face, so they got to come across with pussy.

Why front about it?

So here I come, I cruise on into town, and I whip out my bank, and I'm like: *Yo, either take it or leave it.* Don't mean nothing to me, either way. The bitches, they know the routine. They choose the restaurant. They choose the flick . . . hey, I'll sit through fucking *Waiting to Exhale* for the fucking twelfth time if that's what closes the deal.

Then, it's my time.

You know what's sad? Funny and sad at the same time, I mean? White boys on Saturday night. White boys get slipped a half minute of tongue on a stoop, then come down the steps all smiling—makes me want to go upside their heads! Yo, Biff, you just shelled out a bill on the bitch for a half minute of tongue, and now you're all smiling? What's up with that?

It's like they got no pride, white boys.

I'll tell you another thing about females—I know it ain't what you asked, you can turn off the tape if you want, but it's like a public service thing. The only way a bitch is ever sure you care about her is if you slap her around. I don't mean like pimp-slapping, you know, where you wail on her. It's a wrist thing. It's got to be quick, too, up from the hip in one move, like *pop.* End of story. Then you got to hug her real tight, got to kiss her where hurts. No harm to feel her up either 'cause it gets her blood going—which keeps down the swelling.

The reason bitches go for the rough stuff, no matter what they say, is 'cause it tells 'em they got to you. It's a power thing. I mean, you wouldn't put up with their shit if you didn't care about 'em. You'd just walk away. You know what I'm saying? It's like Nintendo—and for that second, when you're all hugging and sorry, it feels like they've got the stick.

Now I see you're perking up. *Now* I got your attention, am I right? It's like you might think the black man's nothing but an ignorant animal, but when he's talking pussy, even you got to give him his props—mad props, I'm talking, when it comes to pussy. It ain't a dick thing either. I mean, yeah, it *is* a dick thing. But also it's a state of mind. That's what I'm talking about. It's a *mentality.* The black man's got a *mind* for pussy. I'll go you one better. The black man, he *invented* pussy. White folks—with them, well, it's like *intercourse.* Sound like a damn ramp on a highway! It's like, "Oh, Biff, let's climb in the Volvo and have *intercourse."* Then Biff, he's like, "Just a second, Muffy. Let me find my map."

So then the black man comes along, and it's like out of the goodness of his heart, he schooled white boys on how to get nasty. Schooled 'em on how to rock and roll. You know what I'm saying? How to groove, how to work that *thang.* They still ain't got the hang of it, yo, but at least now they're moving in the right direction.

It's the same way with ball. I know a couple of white boys, they got *mad* hops. You know what I'm saying? Crazy mad hops. That flick, *White Boys Can't Jump*—it ain't the truth. White boys can jump. Lots of 'em even got game. It's just that they got game in a white boy kind of way. But they accept it. That's the key. They accept the fact that they ain't never going to be like the black man; they got game but not *game. Flava* is what I'm talking about. The worst thing in the world for white boys is when they try to compete with niggas. It hurts their self-esteem. Be it hoops. Be it pussy. If you a white boy, how you going to compete with the black man? The black man, he's God's own *anointed.* I know it's hurtful for white folks to hear that. But God himself, he anointed the black man, made him in his own image. Made him God on earth. Who do you think made the pyramids? The white man ever make a pyramid? When the white man was still using his own shit to draw dinosaurs on cave walls, the black man, he was building cities. *Cities.* That's what I'm talking about! Cities that make New York and Detroit look like shit stains. The black man, he invented words and language, he invented numbers and calculus. Smart shit like that. Then the white man, he came along and he stole it. Then again, he only stole it 'cause the black man let him steal it. He figured white folks wouldn't survive without it. That's how the black man is, generous with God's gifts. That's how he got himself anointed in the first place. You know what I'm saying?

Next week?

Long as lunch is on you.

Like the saying goes, *You got the dime, I got the time.*

M<small>Y OLD MAN</small>?

Why you want to know about my old man? Didn't I already told you I don't talk to him no more? No, I ain't going to tell you his name. It's his slave name, and it makes me ashamed to say it. Especially since he knows what the white man did to his people. If he was like dumb stupid, well, then I could understand it. But he's smart—he knows stuff, *knowledge* and shit like that. Yo, I'll give the man his props. To take an example, he once broke down that political shit for me—you know, like Republicans and Democrats. You know how he did it?

With a banana!

Man, I'll never forget it. I was like fourteen—no, fifteen. It's November, and he's sitting on the couch, glued to the tube, watching the elections. So I asked him what it's all about—politics, I mean. Why he cares so much since it's just a couple of white dudes. You know what he does? He walks into the kitchen, brings back a banana, and then he hands it to me.

So I'm like, "But I ain't even hungry."

Then he tells me to skip school the next morning, tells me he'll write out a note so I don't get busted, tells me to take the train to Wall Street, find the busiest street corner at noon and eat the banana.

Why I want to do that? I ask him.

But he don't say nothing else. Just tells me to do it.

So the next morning, I'm there. I'm right on the corner of Wall Street and whatever. It's getting near to lunch, and I'm there, and I'm shivering 'cause it's cold, but I got the banana in my knapsack. And I'm waiting and waiting. Then at last it's twelve o'clock, lunch hour, and it's like *pop*—the street's full of suits. You know what I'm saying? Like *pop*! Like one second I'm sitting peaceful by myself, and then a second later I'm surrounded by suits. It's kind of like drowning in a way. I'm drowning in blue and gray, and I got that thing—you know, closetphobia. So I'm like, *Let me eat the damn banana and bounce the fuck out of here.* So I whip out the banana, and I'm about to chow down on it . . . except then I notice something. People are watching me. Before, they weren't paying me no mind. But soon as I whipped out that banana, I'm like the center of attention. Not just watching either. *Staring.* Mad staring. It's like I'm taking a dump or something. But all I'm doing is eating a banana.

That's when it hit me—the reason why people were staring.

It's 'cause they were thinking: *Look at the damn monkey!*

Not just white folks neither. Black folks. Chink folks. Whatever kind of folks came by, they were staring at me, and they were thinking: *Look at the damn monkey with his banana!*

Man, that made me feel bad. You know what I'm saying? Like deep down bad, where it hurts right down inside your stomach. Like getting gut-shot, except worse. I just wanted to toss that banana in the garbage, but I didn't want to stand up 'cause more people would be staring at me. So I'm looking down, you know, chewing fast and just looking down at the sidewalk between my feet, but it didn't do no good. 'Cause I could still feel their eyes, and I could still hear 'em thinking what they were thinking. *Look at the damn monkey!* I ain't never felt time going so slow as the last couple of bites of that banana. So then at last I'm done with it, and I just shove the banana peel in my jacket pocket, and I stand up—and then I realize no one's looking at me no more. It's like as soon as the banana was gone, so was I. Like I wasn't a monkey no more, so I was gone. Like I turned invisible—or like I was the banana peel I just shoved in my jacket pocket.

You know what? That made me feel even worse.

Word!

So I ride the train home, and I wait up the rest of the afternoon for my old man to come home. What I want to know is why he made me go eat that banana in front of all those white folks. Why he made me feel so bad. That's what I want to know.

Well, at last, my old man comes home, and I ask him why he made me do that, why he made me feel so bad. So he says 'cause I asked him about politics. So then he breaks it down for me. He says how America can't deal with the sight of a black man with a banana. He says how white people, they see a black man with a banana, they think *monkey.*

So I say how it wasn't just the white people. How it's the chinks, and even the niggas.

Then he says how that's because the chinks and the niggas pick up on what the white folks think—except he don't say *chinks* and *niggas* 'cause that ain't how my old man talks. He talks kind of white, truthfully.

But I'm getting off the subject.

White people don't want to think *monkey,* he says to me, but yet they do. It's like a culture thing, like something white people live with even if they don't never admit it. Even to themselves. It's like something they're scared of, like a bad dream that got handed down from their ancestors. It don't make 'em bad people, thinking it; it just makes 'em scared people. Scared like maybe,even though they know not to think it, there's something to it? Except that only makes it worse, them being scared of it. Then he smiles at me. The thing is, he says to me, it don't mean nothing. What white people think, what *any* people think, it don't change what a man is. That's what my old man tells me.

Then he came 'round to Republicans and Democrats. It's like this, he says: No one wants to think *monkey,* but they do. Folks that feel bad thinking *monkey,* but think it's their own business what they're thinking, you call them Republicans. Folks that feel bad thinking *monkey,* but want the government to dig down inside their brains and take out what they're thinking, you call them Democrats.

But I'm like, "Why they got to think *monkey?*"

"I just told you," he says. "It's the culture."

"From now on, I see a white boy with a banana, I'm going to think *monkey* at him. See how he likes it."

"That's not the point, Kevin. Do *you* think you're a monkey?"

Naturally, once I grew up, I began to *comprehend.* The reason white folks think *monkey* is 'cause white folks is jealous of the black man. It's like a kind of self-esteem thing—you know what I'm saying? It ain't a culture thing. White folks jealous 'cause of what the black man's accomplished compared to white folks. Did the white man ever get out of slavery? Did he ever invent inventions?

Who invented science?

The black man!

Who invented math?

The black man!

Who invented reading?

The black man!

Who invented medicine?

The black man!

Who invented geography?

The black man!

Who invented music?

The black man!

Naturally, when I talk about what the black man accomplished compared to the white man, I ain't talking about what the white man calls history. You know, like Black History Month shit. George-Washington-fucking-Carver and his peanut. That's what *the white man* says the black man accomplished. That's just bullshit is what that is. What I'm talking about is what came before the white man's history. Before the white man ever came out of his cave. That's when the black man was doing all these things—you know, the things the white man says he did.

The white man's history is stolen history, plain and simple.

But that's the reason white folks look at a black man and think *monkey*—it's 'cause that's about the only way white folks know how to cope. You know what I'm saying? 'Cause they got to look at themselves in the mirror every morning and face the truth. The truth is the white man, he ain't invented *shit*. He tries to take credit for shit, true that, tries to convince himself it was him who really invented inventions, but he's just fronting.

He ain't fooling no one.

That's the reason the black man is an endangered species—'cause the white man is mad jealous of him. Wants him out of the picture. The thing the white man is so afraid of is the black man will come and take his women. Happens all the time. You know how it is. Soon as they get that taste for dark meat, white women I mean, ain't no going back. It's the natural way of the world. Black men and white women . . .

Huh?

Like I said up front—I'm keeping it on the real.

Now maybe you don't like to hear what I'm saying, or maybe I offend your *sense abilities,* or maybe your *thought abilities,* or maybe you plain ain't down with the truth—ain't nothing I can do about that. I'm just bringing it the only way I know how. I'm just reporting reality. You know what I'm saying? I didn't make the world. So I ain't going to shine it up for your sake. What do the spics say? *Ain't my job, man.*

That's the problem with white people. They just don't want to hear the truth. That's the reason they like Jesse so much. What Jesse tells 'em is things are okay, you know, just give us shit like *affirmative action,* and we be cool. We be good negroes. No one get smoked. But when it finally goes down, when our day comes, you think we care a rat's ass about affirmative action? I can see it now. Devils be hiding behind their front doors, whipping out their copies of *The Color Purple* like as if to say: *Look, we down with you, we read Toni Walker!*

That day comes, you wait and see, we be peeling back our share of caps.

What? *Peeling back caps?*

Heh, heh, let's just say it means saying our hellos. Paying respects.

Straight up, though, you got to laugh at 'em—white people, I mean. There was this time, about two years back, I was hanging out 'round midtown, nothing to do, and I decided to hit Playland down at Times Square. Except I got maybe five, six dollars to my name. So I notice this old cunt walking towards me; I think she was coming home from the opera 'cause she's like sashaying up Columbus, and she got that long scarf thing going on, I mean a *fur* scarf, and she's toting one of those square black purses. So I walk up to her, and I say, "Excuse me, miss, I could use a dollar or two—"

Except the words ain't even out my mouth and she's sobbing at me, "Please, take whatever you want, just don't hurt me."

So I'm like, "I ain't ganking you, lady. I could just use a dollar or two—"

But she's still, "Please, oh God please, oh God please . . ."

She's got the tears going too, running down the powder on her cheeks, and I'm waving at her like as if to catch her attention, like as if to say, *It ain't a hold up, you stupid old cunt!* But she's sobbing away, she's peeling off her bracelets and rings, and just then I hear this quiet trickling sound— the old cunt pissed herself! It's dripping down, the piss, like a steady drip, like leaky faucet, puddling up right there between her black shoes. So now I'm watching her piss herself, and I'm like trying to hand her back her bracelets and rings, and she's still shoving the stuff right back at me, still sobbing, still moaning, *Please oh God please oh God please.* Meanwhile, I'm still waving and waving, trying to catch her eye, but I can't get a word in edgewise!

Around now I'm thinking: *How fucked up is this?*

So finally I take the stuff—the bracelets and rings.

Then you know what the cunt says: "Thank you!"
Word up!

The cunt squeezes my hands and says, *Thank you.*

Then she just steps past me, like nothing happened, walks right on by, right on up Columbus, and she don't look back. She's walking funny, shaking her legs, shaking off the piss, but she ain't running, she ain't crying for the cops, she's just walking away . . . like nothing happened, like the nigga up the block didn't just rip her off. So I'm watching her, and I'm like *What's up with that?* But then I feel the bracelets and rings in my palm, and I just kind of shrug, like: *Who cares what's up with that?* So I ran the merchandise over to Herc, who's suitcasing down on 57th and Eighth, and fifteen minutes later, I've got two bills in my pocket.

So me and Herc, we head over to Playland. But now it ain't no good 'cause we keep bagging up—you know, laughing hard, falling off the stick, laughing at the old cunt, how she pissed herself, how she begged me to rip her off, how she wouldn't take no for an answer.

Later on, though, Herc's rolling the situation 'round in his mind. It's around one-thirty in the morning. The two of us are sitting at the edge of the park, right near that statue at Columbus Circle. We just chilling, you know, real mellow—got our Forty Dogs in our laps. But I know Herc's thinking extra hard, cogitating. Strategizing. He's got that far off Herc look on his face, like he's scheming and dreaming.

Then finally he says, "You never *actually* robbed that old cunt."

"That's what I been telling you, nigga!"

"No, you ain't seeing the big picture."

"What big picture?" I ask him.

"You *told her* you wasn't robbing her. But she still *thought* you was."

I don't say nothing, but I got a *Huh?* expression on my face.

"Suppose the pigs pick you up for that," Herc says. "Except now you tell them you wasn't robbing her. You was just asking for a few bucks, you know, like you was panhandling."

"Then the pigs laugh . . . and then they haul my ass to jail."

Herc's grinning at me. "That's why you just a dumb nigga."

"How the pigs not going to haul my ass to jail?"

"'Cause the old cunt's going to back up your story!"

"Why she do that?"

"'Cause it's the truth," Herc says. "You flat out *told* her you wasn't robbing her."

Now I'm beginning to savvy. "So if you *tell* 'em you ain't robbing 'em, then *you ain't robbing 'em* . . . even if they hand over their shit. 'Cause it's like a donation. Which means the pigs can't touch you."

Herc just smiles. "Now who's the Brainiac?"

"You the nigga!"

"Can I get a little love?"

So the next night, me and Herc go cruising down Amsterdam, yo, just two dawgs out for a walk. It's about midnight, or maybe ten minutes after, and we're yay north of that street where Amsterdam hits Broadway—I think it's 72nd Street. Suddenly, up ahead, we notice a couple of fags. Probably, they coming out of the Park. Fags like the park; they like to do their thing behind the bandshell. So now we notice these two fags up ahead of us, and me and Herc just keep walking towards 'em. We don't say nothing, but we both know what's going to happen. So then the fags notice us and stop talking and look down real quick—like how white people do when they're scared. Fags, especially. Plus, these are little fags. The big one's maybe five-seven; the little one's a couple of inches littler. So they're looking down, real quiet, praying we ain't going to hassle 'em. But then we stop right in front of 'em, so they can't walk past, and then the fags look up. Smiling. Like, *Hey, we down with the brothers.*

"We ain't robbing you," Herc says. "This ain't a robbery."

Now they're shaking and quaking—but they're still smiling.

"We was just wondering if you could spare a few dollars."

So the littler fag reaches in his pocket and comes out with a ten, and he hands it to Herc, and then Herc's like, "I do appreciate it."

The littler fag kind of nods at him, still smiling, and then the two of them start to step back, you know, like it's over, but then Herc catches the bigger fag by the arm and says, "My brother," talking about me, "he was, well, kind of hoping for a donation himself."

Now the bigger fag coughs up a Jackson and hands it to me.

Then Herc smiles at 'em. "It's been a pleasure, gentlemen."

So then we let 'em pass, the two little fags, let 'em pass right on up Amsterdam Avenue. Right on their faggy way, safe and sound, you know what I'm saying? Like no harm, no foul. 'Cause we didn't rob 'em. We just, you know, kind of took their donations.

From there, me and Herc figured we'd score a couple of ounces of cheeba. But we ain't got no more than a block or two when we catch a flash of berry. Two seconds later, two of New York's dirtiest hop out, and they pat us down, and then the fatter pig asks us, "Where are you gentlemen headed?"

Now that cracks me up 'cause Herc just called the fags *gentlemen.*

So the fat pig turns to me, and he's like, "Something funny, mister?"

I just shake my head, no.

Then the skinnier pig walks back to the squad car, and then he raps on the passenger window. Then the window rolls down, and who pokes out his head? The littler faggot! He pokes his head out that pig-mobile, and he looks us up and down. Then the fatter pig says to him, "These the two?"

The littler fag nods.

Now the fatter pig turns back to Herc and asks, "Did you just rob these two gentlemen?"

"No sir," Herc says.

"Why are they saying you did?"

"'Cause they lying."

But it didn't do no good. The pigs haul our asses to jail.

So the next morning, me and Herc's standing up in the courtroom. Got our heads down real low, yo, 'cause we know we're in the right, but we figure it ain't going to matter. Except then—what do you know? *Hot damn,* we got a black bitch as our judge! Now she walks in, and we start smiling, just quiet smiling, so no one could see, 'cause we thinking we in like Crisco. So the black bitch starts off talking to the two pigs; then she turns to us. She's looking down at us from behind that desk. She got that robe going on, got that little hammer-thing off to the side. If we see her on the street, we don't look twice. She's just an old black bitch who looks like she ain't been dug out since like before the O.J. trial. Except now she's sitting up there, high and mighty, looking down at us—and, damn, if she ain't looking like Mariah. You know what I'm saying? On the street, I wouldn't have fucked her with Herc's dick. But now, she's looking down at us, and I'm like all cat-eyes.

So now she starts in asking us what happened.

Right off, Herc does the talking. He's telling her how we never robbed those two fags, how we told 'em we wasn't robbing 'em, how they just came across with their money, how it was their own choice.

So the judge, she's busy listening and listening, and me, personally, I'm just thinking, *You go, Herc!*

After Herc's done, the judge turns to me, and she says, "Is that exactly what happened?"

"Yes, ma'am."

Then she's like, "Do you think there was an implied threat?"

"Don't know nothing 'bout no *implied threat,*" I said. It was that shuffling voice I was using, like how niggas used to talk with. "We just asked them for, like, *donations.* You know what I'm saying?"

"Do you represent a charitable organization?"

"No ma'am."

"Then why were you soliciting donations?"

"They gave us that money, ma'am. Just gave it. You know what I'm saying? We didn't rob those . . ." I almost slipped up and called them *faggots,* but Herc, he kind of leaned his shoulder into me, you know, nudging, like to remind me where I was. " . . . *gentlemen.* We didn't rob no one."

"Did you try to intimidate them?"

"No ma'am."

Then the judge waves at the two pigs to come forward, up close, so she can whisper to them. Then she waves forward the Jew we got from Legal Aid, and the other guy, you know, the pig lawyer. So they chatting away, grinning like they all best buds—which, I'm thinking, ain't a good sign. They just chatting away, chatting and chatting. Meanwhile, me and Herc, we're sweating and fretting. 'Cause we both got priors, you know? Mostly j.v. stuff for me, but Herc's got a 211 from when he was nineteen.

Finally, the party breaks up. The pigs and their lawyer go strolling back to their seats. The Jew comes strolling back to us. He's still grinning. Except I don't know if he's grinning 'cause it's good news, or 'cause he's a Jew and he's just sold another two brothers down the river.

So the judge, she hits her hammer a couple of times, and the courtroom gets quiet. Then she looks at me and Herc and says, "Stand up, gentlemen."

I think: Again, *gentlemen!* It's like fucking *Hamlet!*

But me and Herc, we stand up.

"Look at me, gentlemen."

So we look up at her.

"Kevin, I'm going to let you off with a warning. But if I see your face in my courtroom again, I'll be very unhappy. Do I make myself clear?"

"Yes ma'am." I say.

"As for you, Khallid, because the circumstances of the incident are slightly in question, and because you weren't carrying a weapon, I'm going to give you the benefit of the doubt. I'm going to extend your current probation for a period of one year. But if you get in trouble again, things will not go easy. I'm putting my trust in you, Khallid. I'm going out on a limb. Don't make me look like a fool, or there will be a very steep price to pay. Do I make myself clear?"

Herc don't say nothing, just nods.

Now where was I?

So me and Herc, we beat that rap. You know what's kind of funny though? The two faggots, they came up to us outside the courthouse—*and they shook our hands.* Yo, I didn't know if they was dissing us or what. You can never tell with faggots 'cause it's like they got different wiring in their brains. But they didn't *seem* like they was dissing, and besides we was on the steps of the courthouse, so there's pigs everywhere, so we let it go.

That night, though, Herc's still worked up. We on our favorite bench, right off the 97th Street entrance to the park, but Herc, he can't chill. He's like up and down, up and down. Slapping his fist into his palm. "That just goes to show," he says, "you can't trust the devil."

And I'm like, "True that!"

"White man's the *devil.*"

"Word!"

"How you going to trust the devil?"

"Can't do it."

"We never robbed those faggots. We *told* 'em we wasn't robbing 'em."

"Told 'em right out," I say.

"So why they go and lie, say we robbed 'em?" Herc's looking at me. "'Cause they the devil. That's why. Faggots is the devil same as white man's the devil. But they double devils 'cause they faggots *and* they white."

"No doubt."

Then Herc looks at me, kind of a wink look. He pulls his red bandana out of his back pocket and kind of waves it in front of me. "I think we need to take a little walk."

Right off, I know what's on Herc's mind. "No way, son. Unh unh."

"Yeah, a walk would suit me just fine."

"C'mon, Herc. You heard what that judge said."

32

"Damned if I'm going to let no negro bitch tell me when to take a walk," he shoots back. "Take off that robe, she's still just a negro bitch."

The bandshell was quiet when we got there. It was drizzly, you know, like the rain couldn't quite make up its mind to just let loose. The grass was damp and squishy where me and Herc was crouched. And I'm still saying to him how it's a bad idea, what he's got in mind. Which it is. We're there like fifteen minutes, and nothing happens.

"C'mon, Herc," I say. "No one's showing up. It's a signal. Let's roll out of here."

"You do whatever you want . . . *Kevin.*"

The way he said *Kevin,* it was kind of like how that judge said it. Like Herc thought that's who I was. That hurt me. It's like as if he was saying I was still the white man's slave.

Just as I was about to stand up, a couple of fags came walking 'round back. So I drop back down 'cause now I'm in whether I like it or not. I mean, if I rolled out of there, the fags would get scared and maybe bail. Which would piss off Herc even more. Besides, we *didn't* rob those first two fags. So it's not like Herc don't have a point.

For the next couple of minutes, we studying the situation. There was one tall fag, skinny like a broomstick, yo, and real bony, even in his face. He was holding hands with this greasy spic fag—you know the type. He's got that pencil mustache going on, and those seven hairs sprouting on his chin. So you figure the greasy spic fag's *got* to be the one doing the doing, but the next thing you know, it's the broomstick fag on his knees.

Meanwhile, Herc's tying his bandana over his mouth. Which is how I know the talking's done. So now I'm pulling out my bandana, it's red like Herc's, and I'm tying it too.

That's when Herc makes his move.

Those faggots, they don't know what hit 'em. Herc lays out the broomstick fag right off, you know, just takes him down like fucking LT—I mean, that bitch is still slurping and burping as he hits the ground. Then Herc starts wailing on him, you know, *wailing*. You know what I'm saying? He's crazy mad pissed 'cause of what the first two fags did to us, so now he's just *wailing*. Meanwhile, I'm holding down the spic fag. I got him pinned to the ground, face down, and I'm just kind of pushing down on the back of his head, making sure he don't get a good look at Herc.

But then, suddenly, the spic fag's got his right arm loose, and he's reaching back and scratching at me. I mean, just like a bitch! He's scratching the fuck out of me, getting near my eyes—and meanwhile, like I said, all I'm doing is just holding him down. Mind you, I still ain't even hit the cocksucker! That just sets *me* off. So I roll him over, and I'm about to go to town on him. But the second I lean back, yo, he knees me right in the bone. I mean, it's like he might as well *be* a bitch, the way he's fighting.

So I roll off him and turtle up, and he gets in a quick boot, and then another, but just as I'm thinking I'm fucked, I hear Herc swooping in, and about a second later, he's got the spic fag backed up against the bandshell. When I look up, he's going 0-1-2 on the bitch, like *boom, boom, boom*.

I just sit up and watch.

The thing of it is, that spic's a tough little cocksucker. He won't go down. I mean, yo, Herc's saying rights, he's saying lefts—man, he's throwing *bricks*. (Herc onced boxed in the Double G's.) He's coming in with the jabs, one after another. He's got that spic's head's snapping back, slamming backwards into the bandshell, like, *bap, bap, bap*. Herc's got him sagging, you know, hands on his thighs. But the bitch is still standing. In a way, it's like as if he's dissing Herc 'cause he won't go down. But yet you almost got to admire him. I mean, his eyes ain't even in his eyes. He got blood out his mouth, out his nostrils; he even got blood out his left ear, but I think maybe it's just his mouth-blood that splashed up there.

Now Herc's running out of gas.

I stand up and walk over to him.

He's still throwing junk. Not like before, but I can hear the spic's face crack each time Herc lands a solid shot. Nose. Cheekbones. Jaw. It's like wherever Herc lands, something cracks. But finally, Herc's wasted. He steps back and just kind of stares at the spic, then back at me. "What's holding the bitch up?"

"It's a thing."

Herc's kind of shaking his head. "Damn!"

"It's a damn thing."

He looks back at the spic. "I mean *damn!*"

"Word up."

Herc pats his back pocket. "What do you think? Should I cut him?"

I think about it. "What's the point?"

"Well, we can't just leave him like that—standing up."

"Why not?"

"It ain't right. It ain't . . . I mean, it just ain't *natural.*"

"Wait, I got an idea."

Herc backs off, and I walk up to the spic, look him over. He's swaying back and forth, his hands still resting on his thighs. But nobody's home. It's just he's too far gone to know he's still standing. The problem's with his knees. They're locked up tight; he *can't* fall. You know what I'm saying? So I slide in behind him and just basically kick out his left knee. I mean, that spic faggot goes down like he's sawed off.

Then I smile at Herc, and he smiles back at me. Then I'm like, "Now who's the dumb ass nigga?"

Later on that night, after we got washed up, we found us a quiet bench near the reservoir, and we fired up a couple of blunts. Herc ain't said another word about what happened, but I know he's thinking about it. 'Cause I know Herc. You know what I'm saying? I know how his mind works.

So finally I turn to Herc and say, "How bad you think we hurt those two fags?"

"The tall one, not so bad," he says. "But that mother-fucker spic—I think we did him up real good."

"You think maybe the spic's killed?" I ask.

Herc kind of soft-laughs at me. "No way."

I think for a second. "I hope he ain't killed."

"It's his own damn fault; he didn't go down!"

"No doubt," I say. "But I still hope he ain't."

"If it was the other way, you think *his* people be worried about us?"

"I don't mind spics. Some of 'em ain't so bad."

"Spics is just devils who don't talk the language."

"I like spic music."

Herc looks at me strange. "Say what?"

"That Tito Puente shit. I like that."

"It don't even have words!"

"It has words!"

"Not English words!"

"I didn't say English words. I just said words."

"You love spics so much—maybe *you* a spic!"

"I ain't no spic," I say, grinning.

"How I know you ain't no spic?"

"You *know* I ain't no spic."

"Now I see it real clear." Herc starts laughing. "You ain't nothing but a Tito Puente-loving, car-bouncing, burrito-eating spic."

"I like burritos too!"

Herc cracks up hard.

"Maybe I *am* a spic."

"You a freakin' 'Rican is what you are!"

Now I'm cracking up. *"Yo no hablo* fucking *ingles."*

"It's not my *yob,* man!"

Then we laugh some more, then stop. Then it's just the two of us, real quiet.

"All I'm saying is I hope the spic's not killed."

"Whatever," Herc says. "But I'm just saying he could've gone down."

But that's just Herc. Like I said before, he's a crazy mad nigga. Me and him, we real tight. Had us wild times together. You know what I'm saying? Crazy wild times. He's not just a brother, Herc. He's like, you know, a *brother*. Dig! Like my own brother.

What?

Yeah, I got a real brother. But I don't want to talk about him.

Why is it that white folks like yourself are always so curious about fathers and brothers and such? To me, your family ain't the people you're born to; it's the people you choose. Your friends—that's who your real family is. I mean, *dig*. I got *handed* to my old man. You know what I'm saying? No one asked me if I *wanted* him as my old man. No one asked him if he *wanted* me as his son. We just got thrown together. Who knows why?

Now you take Herc—*him* I picked. That makes Herc my real brother. Even if he ain't what *you* would call a real brother, to me, Herc's a realer brother than Dexter ever was. Herc and Jerome and Lakeisha and Fast Eddy and the rest of the One-Forty-Ninth Street Crew. That's who *I* call my family. 'Cause when it comes right down to it, that's who's got my back.

Now Lakeisha, she's a perfect example of what I'm talking about. She once got busy for me after a nappy ho pulled a box cutter. It happened at a barbecue in Fort Hamilton—you know, Crooklyn. Way down near the Verrazano. It was me, Keisha and Eddy. I don't remember where Herc was, but I think it was his friend's yard. The point is, there's lots of niggas I didn't know. But what the hell? Got a DJ jammin' on the one and two. Got ribs. Got slaw. The works. You know what I'm saying? So I'm chowing down, scouting out the local talent, you know, just kind of *reconnoitering,* seeing what develops. Maybe an hour later, I'm headed upstairs with a bitch who called herself Peebo. You ever heard of a name like that? *Peebo?*

That should've tipped me off. She wasn't even *all that* either—like I said, she's a little nappy. But, well, you know, I'd been doing 40's since we got there . . . malt liquors, 40 ouncers. Yo, I was primed to pump. It can't be more than five minutes from the time me and Peebo first hit the stairs till we're in the second floor guest bedroom, bumpin' nasties.

But then, all of a sudden, Peebo goes Mother Theresa on me! I mean, all of a sudden, she's like, *No, stop, we can't do this!* Except I'm just getting the friction on, and it ain't like I'm going to hit the brakes.

But she keeps pushing me off, squeezing her legs together. "Stop!"

"What you talkin' *stop*, woman?"

"Just stop," she's saying. "I don't want to do this no more."

So I'm like, "I ain't playing with you, bitch. Now hold still."

But she's scratching me, biting my lip. She's kicking at my sides. Finally, I just rolled her over her stomach and went back door—it ain't even what I like, but, *fuck,* I was getting the shit beat out of me.

"Motherfucker!" she's screaming. "Motherfucker!"

Yo, I ain't *never* done my business so fast.

Even afterwards, she's still moaning. "Motherfucker."

"What's with you, bitch?"

"You motherfucker," she's crying. "You raped me!"

"Bull*shit* I raped you!"

"You raped me, motherfucker!"

"You a wack bitch is what you are."

"And you a motherfucker rapist!"

Well, I didn't see no point to argue. I just tucked jimmy away and headed back down to the barbecue—just left her there, ass up in the air, like the fucked bitch she was. But I figure I'd better get good and gone 'cause who knew how a ho like that was going to react. Sure enough, it ain't a minute later, I'm on my way out the gate when I hear a noise behind me, kind of *Aaaiiieee!!!* So I turn around, and right as I'm turning, that wack bitch swipes me with a cutter. Wet me across the left pec, but I'm for sure she was going for my throat! Naturally, I grab where I'm cut. I'm like, you know, in shock. For a second, me and Peebo just stand there, just staring at each other; I can feel the blood welling up under my hands. But then she comes at me again. Would've wet me good too—except out of nowhere, Keisha takes out the ho with a brick. I mean, *crack,* right across her ho skull. Peebo's out before she hits the ground, and Keisha's right on her, just to make sure. But then Peebo's homegirl shows up, another nappy bitch, and she's right on Keisha. The two of them start rolling around on the grass, grabbing for the cutter Peebo dropped. Hair ripping out. Clothes tearing off. I must've done Keisha maybe a dozen times, but she ain't never looked as phat as when she was wailing on that homegirl.

Real quick, people's crowding around the two of 'em, yelling their lungs out for the homegirl. I kick the box cutter out of reach so neither of 'em can get it, and then I step back. It's going back and forth, even-steven, for maybe a couple of minutes. They both down to their britches, wailing away, cursing, biting, until the homegirl get in a lucky shot to Keisha's mouth. Knocks out a front tooth— yo, that tooth *shoots* out of her mouth, way up in the air, lands about five feet away on the grass. They both kind of stop to watch it.

That's when a couple of niggas step in and pull 'em apart.

Afterwards, Fast Eddy phones for a taxi, and then him and me wait out front with Keisha. Takes about half an hour. But when the taxi comes, Eddy decides to stick around to make sure there's no hard feelings with local niggas. I tell him there ain't—it's just a bitch thing. It don't mean nothing. But Eddy wants to make sure, so he heads back to the barbecue.

It's just me and Keisha in the back seat of the cab for the ride home. She's got her tooth clutched in her right fist, like she might stick it back in her mouth—that tells me she ain't back in her right mind yet. She's scratched up pretty good. Forehead. Cheeks. The back of her neck. Also, she's got blood on her right tit; I don't know if it's another scratch or maybe a bite. Now I'd have to say, being as objective as possible, homegirl probably got the better of Keisha.

I pull off my windbreaker and wrap it around her.

"You never could scrap a lick," I say real soft.

She smiles back at me, tearing up. "One-Forty-Nine *for life.*"

Now *that's* what I'm talking about when I say "family." You can't *buy* that kind of love. You got to *earn* it. You know what I'm saying? Till the day I die, Keisha's my girl. Yo, she's my blood. My flesh and blood. 'Cause that's what she laid out for me—flesh and blood.

YO, I MADE UP A RAP FOR YOU:

My name's Africa Ali, I'm just 23, but I'm the master key,
And I'm going on a spree, but not with crimes,
'Cause my weapons rhymes, dropping dimes of lines
From time to time, but never mind.
I ain't here to front, so fire up a blunt—I'm going hardcore.
What I live for is what the devils die for, even the score
For Jew slaveships that came before, spilling niggas,
Now we pulling triggas,
Don't feel shit. The lies you taught us about those who bought us,
You cross us, I got my gat between your lips, spitting clips
From the hip till your blood starts to drip.
You fuck with my race,
You face the wrath of the Nubian past—talking 'bout outer-space,
The math of the gods that filled the caves with a pale face, but
The ace of spades whacks diamonds and clubs, drubs the scrubs
That stand in our path. We bury your sons in shallow graves,
Misbehave with your daughters, then drop the bitches in the ditches,
Throw more dirt on the pile—children of the enemy, wait 'n see.
We got to educate the nation 'cause the people got the power,
They just don't know the hour it's all going down. Indignation,
Compensation, time's a-wasting, this dick's for tasting. Niggas
Getting paid, females getting laid, devils be afraid,
Be very afraid,
'Cause I ain't too particular, I'm talking extra-curricular
Activities; I know how to please, so all you fake MC's
Get scratched like fleas, 'cause I'm the big black dog
that howls in the night.
Aa-iight?

41

It threatens you, don't it?

Man, I see that look all the time on white folks. It ain't so much the words; it's the rhythm. It's that jungle beat. It gets underneath your skin, gets you glancing behind you, looking back over your shoulder. You don't know how to deal with it. You're like, *Do I run? Do I dance? Or do I get down on my knees and beg for mercy?*

The thing is, it ain't no *thang.*

It's just free-styling, boy*ee.* Do what you feel! You got to let it talk to you, let it get *into* you, inside your body. You know what I'm saying? You got to listen with your blood. 'Cause that's where rap is coming from. It's the music of the blood. The blood in the street. But yet, if there wasn't no blood in the street, then there wouldn't be no such thing as rap. It would be like it was before, you know, that Frank Sinatra shit. But then rap came along and knocked that mook right off the box. Knocked him right on his doo-bee doo-bee doo-ing ass. You ever heard that song "Doo-bee Doo-bee Doo"? I mean, what's up with that? It makes you want to scream, *Yo, Frankie, just doo-bee doo-bee do the damn bitch already!*

Bone the ho, Frankie!

Say this for Sinatra though. He ran with some stone-cold motherfuckers. I'm talking *stone-cold,* man. Kind of motherfuckers who'd as soon look at you as put a .38 in your skull. Gambino. Traficante. Trigliani. You don't get no more hardcore than that. It's a well-known fact, by the way, that the mafia hired the Jews to invent AIDS. The CIA was in on it too. They were going to use it against Castro, but then a couple of their scuba divers dropped the test tube against a rock off the coast of Haiti. That's how come it spread there first. But once it got going, the government realized what it could do, so then it got spread to Africa. Now the trouble with Africa, from the CIA's point of view, is real simple: too many niggas. So they bring in AIDS, let it do their dirty work.

When the whole AIDS thing is said and done, when the niggas is gone from Africa, you watch the Jews go rushing in and start divvying up all those diamonds.

You ain't Jewish, are you? There's nothing lower than Jews. Not towelheads. Not chinks. Nothing. I hate 'em—bloodsucking bastards! Jew lawyers. Jew doctors. Jew agents. Bloodsuckers, every last one of 'em. It's like that old joke. How do you get a hundred Jews in the back seat of a Toyota?

Throw in a dime.

Go on . . . name me one Jew, just one, who wouldn't sell his mother down the river for a dime. God damn bloodsuckers!

Yo, it's Jews who started slavery; it's Jews who paid off the European kings and queens to send their slave ships to Africa. You know the worst thing about it? It wasn't nothing personal. It wasn't like Jews had something against black folks. They just thought about those African men and women, and about those African babies, and they didn't see people; no, they just saw dollar signs is what those Jews saw.

That's the only thing that gives Jews a hard-on: a dollar sign. So it's like they're sitting in their temples in Europe, thinking about millions of dollar signs running loose in Africa, running around naked and peaceful—and those Jews, they just about creaming in their Jew pants.

Jews always talk about how Hitler killed six million . . . except what they don't never talk about is how *they* killed a hundred million blacks. Or about how there's a hundred million Africans, *kings and queens* I'm talking, buried at the bottom of the Pacific Ocean.

That's how come Jews hate Dr. Jeffries so much. Jerome—that's one of my dawgs—he took a class with Dr. Jeffries up at City College. Now Jerome, he's what you call a scholar. He ain't as street-wise as Herc or me, but that's 'cause he's always cooped up in his room, filling up his brain with books and such. Jerome told me how the rabs and Jew lawyers got together and tried to get Dr. Jeffries fired. You know why? It's 'cause they know that knowledge is power. Word! Jews don't want black folks to know the truth 'cause once you know the truth, can't no Jew lawyer take that away from you.

You got knowledge, you got power.

So it's a power thing with the Jews and Dr. Jeffries. He's a threat 'cause he's up there at City College, you know, twenty-four seven, schooling his students on how white people lived in caves until the black man came along. Just a bunch of shit-sniffing cave boys and cave bitches. That's the ugly truth about white people. It ain't just me saying it neither. It's a certified college professor. Dr. Jeffries, he beat the white man at his own game. He pretended like he was one of them, don't you know, earned his self all their lying white man's degrees, made 'em believe he was just another negro professor. But then, *snap,* he turned right 'round and started to teach the truth.

White folks, they just about had a fit!

White folks like: *Hey, that ain't what we said you could teach!*

Dr. Jeffries, he played 'em!

But, of course, whenever regular white folks get played, the first thing they do is call in the Jews. Who else you going to call when you want to *jew* a black man? It's like in their blood. Jerome told me how the rabs were marching in front of Dr. Jeffries office, how the lawyers were suing the college—or should I say how they were *jewing* the college. It might've worked too. Except then the brothers and sisters stepped up. The black students, I mean. They stood up to the Jews, got right in their faces and said: *That Jew shit don't fly in Harlem-World!* Chased those damn bloodsuckers right back to their temples in Williamsburg.

That's what happens whenever black folks unite. Ain't nothing black folks can't accomplish if we increase the peace.

But the key is Jerome. He was, like, a witness. You know what I'm saying? He saw the whole thing go down. Saw them Jews pack up their beanies and head back to Hymietown. If you want to get the truth out, you got to find witnesses. That was O.J.'s problem. Everybody knows it was the Colombians that wacked that bitch. But O.J., he didn't have no witnesses. The thing about it is, I don't think it was nothing personal—you know, between the Five-Oh and O.J. Nowadays, you hear folks talking how Furman was out to get him, but I think what happened was the bitch got wacked, and then the detectives came in, did their thing, figured out what went down . . . except by then the Colombians were long gone. Normally, no *problemo*. But since it's O.J., well, big *problemo*. 'Cause the Five-Oh ain't going to admit the motherfuckers got away.

So what's left?

Pin it on the nearest nigga!

Actually, in a way, it was lucky O.J. didn't have no witnesses; if he did, the pigs for sure would've gone after some dumb ass nigga scrounging weed down the block. You bet your ass that nigga would be 25-with-an-L right now. But O.J., he was by himself. So it plain *had* to be him. You know what I'm saying? That's when you get Furman with the gloves, Furman with the blood, Furman all over that scene like white on rice. The only reason O.J. got off is 'cause he had the dough to go out and hire himself Mr. Johnnie Cochran.

That's when the regular white folks called in the Jews. It's like I said before. So that Jew bastard, Goldberg, turns around and sues O.J. for money—I mean, how messed up is that? You son gets whacked by Colombians, so you turn around and sue the black man who *didn't* do it. I mean, it was just proved! The glove didn't fit! But that Jew bastard Goldberg, he don't care nothing about who did do it or who didn't do it. He just wants to get paid. 'Cause he's a Jew!

It's funny what happened to O.J., in a way, 'cause he was like my old man's main guy. When I was a kid, growing up, if I'd start talking about Barry or Emmit, all I'd hear was I ain't never seen a *real* running back since I ain't never seen O.J. Used to lord that number over me: "2003!" Even when the damn record got broke, he said it didn't count 'cause the season was longer.

It was like that right up until the trial. What's funny is, for the first time, I felt bad for the nigga—I mean, keeping in mind how the Five-Oh set him up. But not my old man. *He actually believed O.J. did it!* Said he didn't want to discuss O.J. ever again, didn't want to hear the name in his house.

Hey, it was always like that with me and my old man when I was growing up. We'd shoot back and forth, back and forth—I'm talking hours! I'd say Grif, and he'd say Willie Mays. I'd say Shaq, and he'd say Doc. But, truth-fully, I think Dex probably had us both waxed in hoops 'cause he'd say M.J. I mean, yo, even I got to admit, looking back, M.J. is the *Man.*

What?

My brother, Dexter. And I told you . . . I ain't going to talk about him.

Now what was I saying?

You know who my dad's *main* main guy was? Let me give you a hint.

Baseball.

No, not Reggie! My dad didn't give a rat's ass about Reggie!

Jackie Roosevelt Robinson.

That was how he used to say it, real slow and respectful: *Jackie Roosevelt Robinson.* Man, that name brings back memories. Just the sound of it. It's like my old man's voice is inside my brain, saying the words: *Jackie Roosevelt Robinson.* Now the reason my dad made such a big deal about Jackie Robinson is 'cause he said Jackie proved a black man could succeed no matter if white folks didn't want him to. He said Jackie didn't need no help from nobody. Didn't need no public assistance. Didn't need no affirmative action. He just stepped up to the plate and took his swings.

But what my old man didn't comprehend is that times change. Now maybe it's true Jackie got a fair shake back when *he* played ball. But if he came along now, you think the white man would ever give him that chance again? *Naturally,* if you give a brother a fair shake, he's going to outdo the white man. Nobody says no different. But the thing is, that's the main reason black men don't never get no fair shake nowadays. 'Cause the white man wised up.

Still, I don't hold it against him—my dad, I mean. He went to college, got his degrees and shit, but he never got *enlightened* like I did. The education he got was the white man's education. Got taught the white man's truth. Which is false truth. Lying truth. *The white man did this. The white man did that.* That's the white man's history, plain and simple. You crack open the white man's history books, what do you find? The white man sailing all over the world. Discovering places. Inventing things. You got to be *enlightened* to know it's nothing but lies. With all his so-called education, my old man never learned how the black man built the pyramids. Or how the black man taught the white man to sail his ships using stars to guide him. Or how the white man got the idea of Christmas from Kwaanza. What the white man did to my father was he stole his *pride.* You know what I'm saying? I mean, by the time he graduated college, my old man didn't know nothing about his own people. He wasn't *prideful* like he should've been. Like every black man should be. 'Cause his ancestors, they were *kings and queens.* Except my old man don't even know it!

Yo, I can't never forgive what the white man did to my father!

Would've done it to me too. It could've happened. Except I lucked out with a couple of school teachers—you know, it only takes one or two brothers to undo the lies of the white ones. The first was fifth grade. Name was Mr. Gerhard. Mr. Gerhard gave me a book called *Know Yourself*—I still got that book somewhere. It taught about how the ancient Africans had secret knowledge and power, how they ruled the whole damn world—like I've been telling you. It's where I learned about levitation and such.

Then I had Mr. Joseph in seventh grade. The thing is, that was the year I got held back—mainly 'cause I began to realize that what I was learning was white lies. I mean, I wasn't going to write down white lies in my notebook. So after I got held back is when Mr. Joseph came along, and he kind of took me under his wing. I'll never forget it. He told me to stay after class on a Friday—I remember it real clear 'cause it was a like the last warm Friday of the year, and I just wanted to get out to the court and hoop it up. But Mr. Joseph, he walked me back to his office, shut the door, sat me down—and, *man,* he just got right in my face.

"What's your problem, boy?" he said.

So I'm like, "Don't you call me *boy!"*

But he don't bat an eye. "I'll call you *boy.* I'll call you *nigger.* I'll call you *shit-for-brains* if I take a mind to do it!"

Yo, if he wasn't a black man, I would've laid him out!

"You just like the rest of 'em," I yelled. "You against me just like them."

Then he starts laughing. "And you just figured that out now?"

Now *that* kind of catches me off guard—'cause it's the first time I ever heard somebody admit it.

"Boy," he says, "this is *America.* You are a black man in *America."*

"So what?"

"So you were born behind the eight ball. Do I have to spell it out for you?"

Meanwhile, I'm just staring at him.

"Boy, this ain't your country. It ain't never going to *be* your country—unless you make it your country. What? You think white folks are going to turn over their country to the likes of you? White folks are going to fight to keep what's theirs the same way you or I would fight to keep what's ours. They're going to fight you day in and day out, fight you tooth and nail, however they can. They're going to fight you with ignorance in your classrooms, with intimidation in your jobs, with injustice in your neighborhoods. So either you fight back, or you might as well surrender right now—and shuffle on out of here."

"I ain't scared of no white man!"

"Then you've got to beat him at his own game! Do you understand what I'm saying to you, boy? You've got to know his rules, you've got to practice his ways. Then you've got to go out and do better than him. You've got to think faster, you've got to work harder, you've got to learn more. That's the only way to get ahead in a white man's world."

After I got home, I told my old man what Mr. Joseph said to me. But he just kind of rolled his eyes. Except I found out the next day he called the principal and tried to get Mr. Joseph fired! Looking at it one way, I can sort of see where he was coming from, my old man, 'cause you don't want no one disrespecting your own flesh and blood. But looking at it another way, he tried to get a *brother* fired. Man, you don't never do that—especially if all the brother did was speak the truth! You know what I'm saying? I don't think I was ever more ashamed of my father than I was right then; it felt almost like *he* was white. Like he didn't want me to find out the truth, like he was helping the white man hide the truth from me! Like he'd gone over to the other side!

The thing is, it didn't take no more than a week before what Mr. Joseph told me began to hit home. I had a test in . . . what do you call it? Maps and shit. What? Geography. Yeah, but that wasn't what it was called. Social studies. That's it. I had a big test in social studies. So I kept in mind what Mr. Joseph said, and I read on it like nobody's business. Crazy mad books! You know what I'm saying? So then the big day comes, and I'm right in the front row, and the bitch teacher hands out the test—and there ain't one single answer I know. It's like the bitch looked inside my brain, saw exactly what I didn't know, and put that on the test! I wound up getting a fifty-three. I mean, *damn*. Fifty-three!

So I walked up to the bitch afterwards, and I asked her how come she gave me a 53.

You know what the bitch says?

"Because that's the grade you earned, Kevin."

So I'm like, "But I know the shit!"

Then she says, "I'm sure you'll do better on the next test."

Meanwhile, there was a white kid who sat next me— Blake. I still remember his name 'cause I used to gank him up for coins. He wasn't no Urkel either; I mean, I *knew* I was smarter than that kid. So I go up to him the next morning and ask him what he got on the test. You know what he tells me?

Eighty-eight!

The second he said eighty-eight is when I realized it's even worse than what Mr. Joseph said. It's like he cut the product 'cause he thought I was still too young to hear it hardcore. Left mc to figure out the rest by myself:

It don't matter how hard you work. The white man ain't going to let you get ahead.

Yo, it was like a *realization*. Like when you open a window on a cold night, and the cold air just blows against your face. So right off, I wailed on Blake. Beat the shit out of his eighty-eight-getting ass. Wound up in the counselor's office, but I didn't listen to a word the cunt was saying— 'cause I knew it was more trip. All I could think about was how a black man don't stand no kind of chance in the white man's world. I'd have to say that was the exact moment I became one of the Five Percent Nation.

I know. I'll break it down for you.

Take a group of people. Could be black people, could be white people—it don't make no difference. You got three types inside that group. First, you got the eighty-five percent that's basically ignorant. Don't know what the fuck is going down. Too busy keeping on keeping on. Then you got the ten percent that got fake knowledge and use it to suck the blood of the eighty-five percent. Last, you got the five percent. The five percent got true knowledge, so it's their job to save the eighty-five percent from the ten percent; the only way to do that, to save 'em from the ten percent, is to lead by example. That's what you got today in the black community. You got the Ten Percent Nation, bloodsuckers of the poor—I call 'em negroes—warring against the Five Percent Nation.

Except it ain't a war with bullets—not yet!

It's a war of words.

That's what rap is.

It's the words we fire off instead of bullets.

People say the white man's the devil—which is true. But when you get right down to it, the worse devil is the one you can't see. It's like, you can *see* the white man for his ugly self. But the ten percent, the bloodsuckers, what makes them so dangerous is they look like us. Well, not like you. But, looking at a black man, it's hard to know what kind of percenter he is. It ain't like Bloods and Crips where you got colors to go by. You know what I'm saying? It's a *psychological* thing. You got to listen to what a brother's saying. You got to *hear* his rap. Not just listen to it. You got to hear it with your mind.

YO, I WAS TALKING ABOUT YOU A COUPLE OF DAYS AGO.
Word!

Me and Jerome, we was sitting around his place, you know, just chilling, just conversating. So I told him about how I was getting interviewed. Well, he just looks at me strange at first. Then he asks me what for I was getting interviewed, and I told him for writing articles, and he asks me what kind of articles, and I said I don't know—but what difference it makes?

He thinks on that for a minute.

Then he's like, "Why you want to talk to some Caucasian?"

Seemed kind of jealous truthfully. Jerome's like that. Don't like no one but him to get noticed.

So I'm saying again, "What difference it makes?"

"That Caucasian paying you?"

I just shake my head, no.

"Then why you talking to a Caucasian man who ain't paying you?"

Now I'm thinking for a minute. "Ain't no reason not to."

Then Jerome just kind of smiles. "You know what you are?"

"What?"

"Nothing but a lab rat. That's what you are," he says.

"I ain't no lab rat."

Now he smiles even bigger. "Lab rat for the Caucasian."

"I *ain't* no lab rat!"

"Maybe, after you finish up talking, that Caucasian make you run 'round and 'round on one of those lab rat wheels."

Now I *know* I ain't no lab rat. You and me, we both know that. It ain't even an issue—you know what I'm saying? Except Jerome, well, he kind of started me thinking. Like maybe you and me could work out something. Like, you know, an arrangement? It's like that old saying. Time equals money. So I was just thinking, you know, since I'm giving you my time . . .

What?

No, I ain't saying *that*. I ain't saying I won't do it no more. Talk, I mean. It ain't like I'm shaking you down. Look, I want to get the truth out as much as you do. I'm just saying I was talking to Jerome, and he kind of got me thinking. That's all I'm saying.

Besides, I ain't into all that material shit. I figure you ain't got nothing, yo, you got nothing to lose. Word up! That's what the Koran teaches. You could look it up. I got friends can't scrounge bills for an eight-ball—but come the weekend, niggas be Benzin' up Broadway. That's one of the main ways the white man keeps us down. Gets us focused on Benzes and GT's and such. It's like *materialism*—that's one of the few things the white man invented by himself. But I ain't into no white man's materialism. Sometimes I see one nigga shaking down another nigga for a pair of damn Nikes, and I just want to grab him by the back of the neck and say, "Yo, why you don't just go out and do the devil's work for him?"

Me? What do *I* do?

Heh, heh, well, you know, a little of this, a little of that. But then again that ain't what you're *really* wondering about, is it? So why don't you just come on out with your question?

Yeah, I deal.

Been doing it since I was seventeen. Even before that, I curried for a couple of brothers who lived on my block. The thing is, it ain't even a thing. You know what I'm saying? It's like the so-called *underground economy,* like I got a corner store, you know, like mom and pop. Except instead of gumballs and such, I move weed. But I don't go nowhere near crack. Never have, never will. 'Cause crack is a plague on our community.

Now Herc, he says I'm dumb stupid. Says that's where the real duckets is—crack, he means. So I tell him about how crack is a plague, and I know deep down he's bugging about it, but meanwhile he just keeps on keeping on. The thing about Herc is he does lots of shit he don't want to do, not in his heart of hearts, shit that he knows it ain't right. The reason is 'cause Herc don't like himself. He don't have the self-esteem. You know what I'm saying? If he had the self-esteem, like how I do, then it's for sure he wouldn't deal crack.

Ain't worth the effort besides—crack, I mean. Herc tells me about the dudes he does business with. Not the buyers, mind you. I'm talking the suppliers. Badass motherfuckers, you know, the kind Don Corleone shits himself thinking about. I'm talking Caucasians with like horn-rimmed glasses and twitches and briefcases. The kind of badass motherfuckers you don't never want to mess with.

No thank you.

It's like the song says: *You got weed, you got what you need.*

Now what that means is if you got weed, you got whatever. Bitches. Bank. What have you. You just got to know how to work it, if you catch my drift. Even the pigs don't hassle you for weed . . . unless of course they take a mind to hassle you, but then it don't much matter 'cause they're going to hassle you regardless. What I'm saying is since I don't go near crack, it's almost like me and the pigs got our signals worked out. They roll up on my corner, I don't make a move. I don't run. I don't do nothing except just stand there. Nine times out of ten, some fool nigga down the street's already bailing.

Pigs chase his ass right past me, and meanwhile I'm just grinning, nodding, minding my own business. It's like a joke to me. Pigs be chugging with their arms, be panting, out of breath, running off after a stringbean nigga holding a rock and a zootie.

I can laugh at it, don't you know, 'cause I don't take it personal.

That's the key to the whole thing—don't take it personal. That's the key, right there, in a nutshell. If a pig pats you down for no reason, well, you know, he's just being himself. Which is a pig. It ain't nothing personal. Ten minutes ago, he didn't know you. Ten minutes from now, he ain't going to remember you. That's why I almost kind of blame Rodney King for what happened to him. I say to him, "Yo, Rodney, you're a black man in a sports car. Sooner or later, you're going to get pulled over. It's going to happen. So why take it personal? That just gives the motherfuckers an excuse to go to town." What Rodney should've done is just grinned and then, after the pigs left, tore up the ticket.

You can't take it personal, Rodney.

You know who's another example of a brother who took it personal? Spree is who. Latrell Spreewell. He choked that cracker coach of his out at Golden State. Ain't no point to it is what I'm saying. You're pulling down the notes, why go after a cracker coach? That don't mean you have to take it if you're getting disrespected. But there's ways and then there's *ways*.

Now if I was Spree, here's what I would've done. First, I would've gone out and hired me a Jew. Then I would've asked for a trade . . . except ain't no way I'm going to be traded 'cause I'm Spree. I'm like the whole team. So then I tell my Jew to tell management it's either me or the coach.

You think that cracker coach is worth 25 a game?

Next thing you know, cracker's back in Arkansas.

Now *that's* how you get things accomplished!

So the moral of the story is like I said: you can't take things personal. That's the trouble with females when you get right down to it. Like Tanya, when she was nagging me to say I loved her. Even Lakeisha's like that. It's like she's on her period except it's not her time of the month. It's like a brain period, like she needs a tampon between her ears. That's the main reason I don't do her no more. 'Cause she always takes it personal. The last time I did Keisha was almost a year ago. It was a weeknight, maybe a Tuesday or a Wednesday; I was out clubbing with Fast Eddy, you know, gaming the bitches, but I'm getting nowhere. It was just one of those nights—you know what I'm saying? I'm talking smooth, breaking lines like a butter sandwich, but it ain't doing no good.

So pretty soon it's going on two in the a.m., and Eddy's bugging to bounce, saying how he's got to wake up early for work. But it's like a nine dollar cover at the place we was at, so I'm saying, *Yo, dawg, just another hour.* But then I turn around and he's gone. Just up and ditched me. Which is the reason why we call him Fast Eddy. Now I got no ride home, and it's two trains I got to take. And I'm like looking around, sizing up the situation, and I realize there ain't a ho left in the joint even worth a chickenhead. You know what that means, *chickenhead?* Well, that's when I decide to call Keisha. The main reason is because her sister's house is a five minute bus ride from the club, so I don't got to deal with the subways. But then again I also figure I'll do her— so at least I don't wind up, you know, all *edgy* the next morning.

So I beep her from a phone outside the club; I almost called her direct, but I didn't want to wake up her sister. Three minutes later, she calls back, and I ask her straight out if she's up for a booty call. I could've scammed her, but it's Keisha, so I just asked her straight out. Then she's thinking for about minute, yawning, bitching how she's going to have to shower.

But I'm like, *Hey, Keish, it just me!*

That's when she starts smiling; it's like she's been down with me for so long I can *hear* her smiling over the phone.

"I know who it is, fool!"

"I'm just looking to get in, get busy, and then get to sleep."

"You can't ask me no nicer than that?"

"I ain't going to disrespect you with no sweet talk, bitch!"

When I show up at her house, she's waiting inside the front door in her red silk robe. She slides the door open real slow, and then she's like "Shhh!" 'cause her sister and her niece is still asleep upstairs . . . which cracks me up for some reason. Maybe it's 'cause Keisha is about the loudest bitch I ever did fuck, and I know, likely as not, we going to wake up the whole damn neighborhood. But now I'm playing along, and I'm like "Shhh!" back at her, and then, as we get to the stairs, I'm like "Shhh!" again.

Then we walking upstairs, and I say, "You looking *phat*, girl!"

"That sound like sweet talk to me!"

"Maybe so, but it's the plain truth."

She's starts laughing, a soft kind of laugh. "You so full of shit!"

Then I slap her right on the ass.

"T-t-t-tootsie roll!"

She jumps up a couple of steps.

"Got to get me some of that . . . t-t-t-tootsie roll!"

She takes off and runs on up the last five steps, *boom, boom, boom, boom, boom* and then runs real fast into her bedroom, and meanwhile I'm one step behind her. She dives onto the bed, and the red silk robe flies up like Superman's cape—and that's when I see she ain't got on her regular underwear. Just a thong kind of thing, dark red like the robe. Now that booty's just calling out to me, just calling out my name, saying: *Knock da boots, Africa! Knock da boots, boyee! Knock da boots!* So now I start in kissing on her, and at first she's kissing me back, but then, suddenly, she's shoving me away.

"Yo, nigga, you got mad stank breath!"

"Who you saying got stank breath?"

"You do, nigga. *Mad* stank breath."

Then I'm like smiling. "What kind stank breath?"

"Mad," she says. "Stank like gin and vodka."

She rolls backwards and reaches into the drawer of her night table, and then she comes back with a roll of peppermint Certs. So I chomp down on like six of 'em at once, and meanwhile, Keisha's sitting real patient on the edge of the bed. It's kind of comical when you think about it. She's sitting on the edge of the bed, and I'm sucking and chomping half a dozen peppermint Certs. Finally, I swallow hard a couple of times, and then I reach for her arm. "C'mon over here, bitch."

She smiles. "Now I ain't even in the mood."

I smile back at her. "T-t-t-tootsie roll!"

"Shhh!"

Then I yank her back down onto the bed.

The red thong don't last but another minute.

So now the thong's off, and the two of us is naked, getting busy on that bed, gnawin' and clawin', and she's still *Shhh!* and I'm still *Shhh!* But then I feel her legs come 'round my hips—which is what Keisha does when she's revving up. I got just enough time to get out one last *Shhh!*

Then it starts.

"Fuck me, you cocksucker! Fuck me, honey nigga!"

"Shhh!"

"Fuck me with that fucking nigga cock of yours!"

"Shhh!"

"Keisha needs her some of that fine nigga cock!"

"Damn, Keish—"

"That's it, motherfucker! That's it! Now you're fucking me!"

"Shhh!"

"You're fucking me! You're fucking me! You're fucking me!"

Now all of a sudden I hear her sister pounding on the bedroom door, yelling "What's going on, Keisha?" and "Damn it, Keisha, open the door!" So I'm trying to focus, you know, trying to seal the deal and get out as quick as I can. Except then I hear the niece, who's like six years old, and she's knocking on the door too, crying "Somebody's killing Auntie K! Somebody's killing Auntie K!"

So now I got that in one ear, and in the other ear I got, "You're fucking me!"

"Shhh!"

Then I panic. I don't know what else to do, so I start slapping Keisha's face.

The crazy bitch just grabs my hand and starts sucking on my fingers.

Now I hear the sister again. "Answer me, Lakeisha! Who's that in there with you?"

Finally, I call out, "It's just me, Vanessa. It's Africa."

"Africa?" she says. "How long you been in there?"

Keisha's squeezing me so hard with her legs I barely got air to answer. "Not too long. Maybe five minutes."

Then I hear the niece again. "Why's Africa here, momma?"

"It's all right, baby," Vanessa says. "Let's go back to sleep."

For half a minute, it gets real quiet. Just the sound of Keisha sucking on my fingers.

Then I hear Vanessa's voice back outside the door. "I'll deal with you in the morning, slut."

Suddenly, Keisha spits out my fingers. "Who you calling slut?"

But Vanessa's already gone.

Now I'm shaking my head. "*Damn,* woman! Why you got to get so noisy?"

She smiles at me kind of sly. "I don't get so noisy with Jerome or Eddy."

Right off, I don't like the tone of her voice. "What you saying, Keisha?"

"Just that Jerome and Eddy don't do for me like you do for me."

"How I know you don't say the same exact thing to Jerome and Eddy?"

"'Cause I don't," she says.

"But how I *know* you don't?"

Keisha thinks on that for a couple of seconds, then grabs the cell phone from the night table. "You can call 'em up and ask."

"It's three in the morning, bitch!"

She grins at me. "Well, that ain't my fault."

The way she's grinning at me kind of pisses me off— like she's so for sure I ain't going to do it, like I ain't going to call nobody at no three in the morning. Except what she don't realize is I was out clubbing with Fast Eddy. So she hands me the phone, and I take it, just grinning back at her, and then I dial up Eddy. But Keisha, she's cool. She just keeps on grinning. I *know* she thinks I'm going to hang up before he answers, but meanwhile I'm just sitting there, on the edge of the bed, listening to the phone ring and ring. Finally, after about ten rings, Eddy picks up the phone.

"What up, dawg!" I say.

Eddy don't know if he's dreaming or what. "Kevin?"

"What up!"

"What time is it?" he asks me.

"'Round three in the morning."

"You in trouble?"

"Nah, I'm in Keisha's bed."

Eddy starts laughing. "You calling me for instructions?"

"Why I call *you* in that case? You the last nigga I call!"

"You high?"

"Not no more," I say. "Not since over an hour ago."

"Then why'd you wake me up?"

"Keisha say I do her different than you and Jerome—"

"*For* me!" Keisha says in my ear. "Do *for* me."

I say, "What?"

"What I said was they don't do *for* me like you do for me."

So I'm like, "I don't even know what you talking 'bout, bitch!"

Then I hear Eddy in my ear: "What she means is she ain't in love with me and Jerome like she's in love with you."

Soon as I hear what Eddy said, I feel kind of a sick feeling down in my gut. I pretend like nothing's wrong, I don't even look up, but deep down inside my gut, all of a sudden, I know it's true. It just never hit me before. The fool bitch *loves* me! So right then and there, I know I got to get out—get out of that bed, get out of that room, get out of that *predicament.* That's the only word for what it was. It was a predicament. You know? It was a predicament 'cause, on the one hand, boning a bitch that loves you is *asking* for trouble. It's like *begging* for trouble. But yet, on the other hand, it wouldn't be right just to haul ass 'cause, well, it's *Keisha.* You know what I'm saying? That's my homegirl. My homegirl out of *all* my homegirls.

So what do I do?

Then, all of a sudden, I got the answer: *Pass the fuck out!*

It's like one second I'm grinning at her, grinning and thinking, "What do I do?" Then the next second, I drop down onto that mattress like I got shot. Just *whap!* You ever seen that video of the Vietnam chink, the one where the Vietnam sergeant blows his brains out? That was how I hit that mattress. I could've won a damn Oscar award. Just let go of the telephone and then *whap!* right down on the mattress. Eyes shut. Mouth open. Just *whap!*

I hit that damn mattress, yo, and I didn't move. Didn't blink. Didn't twitch. Just breathed real slow in and out. After about five seconds, I hear Eddy's voice coming from the phone saying "Kevin? You there, Kevin?"

Then I feel Keisha shoving my right shoulder a couple of times and kind of giggling. "Africa?"

Finally, I hear Eddy's voice again. "Somebody talk into the damn phone!"

That gets Keisha's attention. She picks up the phone and says, "You still there, Eddy?"

Then she starts laughing.

"Straight up, Eddy," she says. "The nigga's flat out. Just passed flat out on the bed. I ain't never seen nothing like it."

She and Eddy's having a good laugh. Even I'm kind of smiling underneath my mouth.

"Well, then, since you the one was out with him," Keisha's saying, "then I guess it your damn fault. What the hell you been pouring down my honey nigga's gullet?"

The two of them, they just laughing and laughing. I figure ain't nothing left to do but lie still and go to sleep.

Which is what I do.

Come the next morning, I get waked up by the sound of yelling and cussing down the hall. Keisha and Vanessa going at it pretty good. That's my cue to hit the road. I don't even stop to pee. Just yank on my clothes fast as I can and scoot down the stairs. Almost made a clean getaway— except, at the bottom of the stairs, I run into Keisha's niece. She's looking up at me all scared and watery 'cause of all the screaming upstairs.

So I like pat her on the head. "It don't mean nothing, kid. Take it light."

She kind of smiles at that, and I start walking towards the door.

"Was you the one fucking Auntie K?"

Well, that just cracks me up. I pick her up so I can look her right square in the face.

"Let's keep that a secret," I say to her. "Just between the two of us, all right?"

"All right," she says.

Then I set her down, pat her on the head again.

"We cool?"

Now she's smiling. "Yeah, we cool."

Cute little bitch.

Testing one . . . two . . . three . . .

Hello?

My name is Lakeisha M.Young, and I am a proud black female. I *know* who I am. You know what I'm saying? So first off I just want to say *One-Forty-Nine for life!* You know what I'm saying? *For life!* Africa. Hercules. Eddy. Jerome. Yo, you *know* I got your back, niggas! Y'heard? Big ups to my big sister, Vanessa. And to my niece, Janine. And to my crucial ho's: Taisha, Dorinda, Mona Lisa and Caramel.

What up, y'all!

All right, now you can ask your questions.

What?

Africa say you want to talk to me. What you want to know?

Well, if you don't got no questions, then why you waste my time? You don't think I got nothing better to do except eat lunch with some sweater-wearing, pony-tailed white man? I took two trains to get here! Not to mention I don't even like chink food. So unless you got questions, I'm out.

What? How I feel about Africa?

Why, he my honey nigga, fool! That mean, first of all, he my nigga. Like, I'm down with him. But also he my *honey* nigga. The rest of 'em, Herc and Eddy and Jerome, they just my niggas. You know, my crew. But Africa—he my honey nigga. I don't know how to explain it no clearer.

Ask me something else.

How I think he feel about me?

I'll say it right out: *Africa love me.*

Naturally, he won't never admit it. 'Cause he's, like, scared. Not scared like you be scared of a *thing.* You know what I'm saying? Like you be scared of a ghost or a skeleton. But scared in his heart. See, Africa—he sexed a lot of so-called women. Except when I say *women,* I mean like bitches and ho's. You know what I'm saying?

What?

No, not like Mona Lisa and Caramel!

When I call them ho's, what I mean is they *my* ho's. Like they down with me, so I call 'em my ho's. But it don't mean nothing. It like when I call Africa my nigga, I don't mean nothing bad by it.

Now where I was?

Oh, yeah. I was saying how Africa scared of what he feel for me 'cause he ain't never had no real *relationship.* You know what I'm saying? He ain't never known what it like to wake up next to a good woman . . . a *lady,* to coin a phrase. I mean, I *know* my shit is prime. You know what I'm saying? But Africa, he been too busy skanking around, sexing his bitches and ho's. I don't blame him for doing that 'cause he just a man—I mean, basically, every man a hound dog. But Africa, he got a good soul, the kind of soul that get lonely in the middle of the night. You know what I'm saying? So I can't really hold it against him—the skanking around, I mean.

That don't mean I *like* it. When I found out Africa sexed Caramel, yo, I near tore that bitch's hair out. But then a week later, me and her down again. 'Cause she knew where I coming from. It's like, I might give it up for Raheem—that Caramel's man—for one night. But it don't count for nothing 'cause I know Raheem belong to Caramel. The way I look at it is if Africa out sexing up Mona Lisa or Caramel, he ain't sexing up no strange Bronx slut who might give him Lord knows what. AIDS or shit. So in other words, if he ain't being with me, I'd rather he being with Mona Lisa or Caramel or even Taisha. He ain't never sexed Dorinda though—which is luckily for her 'cause I know she always deep down want to get next to him.

What you got to understand is black folks look at sex different from white folks. For white folks, sex is like *Sex.* Like with a big old S. You know what I'm saying? But for black folks, sex don't come with no big S. It just, you know, sex. It what folks do in the natural way of things. Black folks just more natural how they live than white folks. It in our blood to be that way. Come from running 'round naked back in Africa. It just how we feel. You know what I'm saying? It how we feel about our bodies, about natural shit.

You know where you can tell the difference? In the bootie. Just think about it for a minute. Bootie the most natural thing in the world. But white women got no bootie. Or else the ones that got bootie, they weigh like 250 pounds. But your average white woman, like for example the ho from Baywatch—you know, Pamela. She got fly titties, but no bootie. It ain't *natural.* You know what I'm saying? What good titties without bootie?

Like a damn Barbie doll.

You ask Africa if I'm lying. Like I said, he a hound dog. Been with lots of women, even a couple of white women. But he always come back to me. 'Cause he need a real woman, not no Barbie doll.

That how come he my honey nigga.

What?

He told you about Tanya? That kind of surprise me 'cause he don't talk on her too often.

No, Tanya ain't white!

But since you brought up the subject, I'll tell you straight out about Tanya. Straight out and for real. That the worst bitch Africa's ever got with. Bar none. You know what I'm saying? *Bar none.* The meanest bitch, the nastiest bitch, the plain old bitchiest bitch that ever was. Me and her almost got down a couple of times. It luckily for her Africa always around to save her bitch ass, 'cause I swear to God I would've took her out. You know what I'm saying? I would've cut her for real.

Why?

Well, it ain't so much what she said or did. It what she is—you know what I'm saying? Which is a twenty-four seven bitch. When she first got next to Africa, it like she

65

didn't show nobody no respect. Not Herc. Not Jerome. Not Eddy. The first time I laid eyes on her, it was at a club on First Avenue—I don't remember the name. It on 103rd Street, though, up in East Harlem. *Dag,* it right on the tip of my tongue—the name, I mean. It don't matter. Africa told us he bringing his new lady that night. Except she didn't show until midnight. Now, personally, I think she was turning tricks back then. So she come waltzing in at midnight, just strutting around like she all that. Which she ain't by the way. She got a nice face—I'll give her that. But she got her hair all straight like she want to be white. Plus, she got no meat on her. Shaped like a ten year old white boy. So in she strut, queen of the world, and she walk right up to the two of us—me and my honey nigga. She walk right up to the two of us *while we dancing,* and she just start to stare. Don't say nothing. Just stare.

Now Africa, he got his back toward her. Don't even know she right behind us. But I noticed her, like I said, the second she strut through the door—except I don't even know who the hell she is. All I know, she staring me down, and so meanwhile I'm staring her down too. 'Cause I don't take that from no ho. Not no how. So the jam pumping, and I'm still staring her down, and she staring me down, and then the music stop, and that when I step up and say to her: "Yo, bitch, you got a problem?"

She pretend like she don't even hear me.

Well, that when Africa turns around.

"Yo!" he say. "Yo, Tanya! You late!"

Right off, from the sound of his voice, I know I can't wax her ass.

Then she like, "Who's that woman you're dancing with?"

Suddenly, Africa get all smiley. "That? That just Keisha!"

Ain't never had no word hurt me so much as that *just.*

"I don't like it here," she say, real dainty. "It's too loud."

So I say, "Maybe you don't like music."

Then I get the stare again. "Maybe I don't like *cartoon* music."

I ain't never wanted to wax a bitch so bad!

But Africa, he just smile stupid and take it. He start pulling her out onto the dance floor. But she shake free—and then, next thing you know, she strutting right out the door.

So I say, "Let the ho go!"

Except Africa don't even hear me. He halfway out the door, running after her like she all that, like her cunt don't stink. Which I'm sure it does from when she was turning tricks.

So that Tanya's story.

Now the question you probably ask yourself is why Africa would mess with her in the first place—why *anyone* would want to mess with a nasty old stank-cunt like Tanya. Well, it a good question. The thing is, Africa does shit sometimes just to like punish his self. You know what I'm saying? It like he's still mad at his self 'cause of what happened with his brother. . . .

What?

You going to sit there and tell me he told you about Tanya, but he didn't tell you about Dexter? That don't make no sense! But, in a way, it just go to show my point. He ain't, you know, *rational* about shit. . . .

No, I ain't going to tell you what happened with Dexter! If Africa want you to know about it, he told you his self. Which he didn't. So he must not want you to know.

I ain't saying another word on the subject.

The point I was making was Africa wouldn't never've gone for no skanky bend like Tanya except 'cause he hurting deep down inside his self. See, when you don't respect yourself, you do shit you wouldn't do if you did. That the reason why we got to teach the children to respect their selves. . . .

What?

Naturally, I respect myself. Like I said, I am a proud black female. I know who I am.

I didn't used to though. Yo, there was a time I did all kinds of bad shit until I learned to respect myself. Evil shit. You know what I'm saying? Shit I wouldn't never do if I respected myself. When you don't got no respect for yourself, well, it work on your mind. Get you all twisted 'round inside till right seem like wrong and wrong seem like right.

Don't rush me! I'm getting to it. But you got to build up to shit. You know what I'm saying? You got to build up so folks stay interested. You got to tease before you please.

It was about three years ago. No, four years ago 'cause I just graduated high school. But what I didn't learn in school was how to respect myself. How to know who I am. How to hold my head up high as a proud black female. *That,* I never learned in school. School only ever taught me to hate myself. To hate myself and my people.

So I was eighteen years old, and I had a friend name Brianna. We real tight, me and Brianna—even though she two years older than me. She used to score me weed since her man a dealer. Nothing big. Just small time. Marcus was his name—Brianna's man, I mean.

So far, so good.

The problem was Brianna had a daughter. Baby girl with great big brown eyes named Chanelle. So Bri used to call me up in the middle of the night to come get Chanelle 'cause Marcus starting in on her, and once Marcus got started in on Bri, he sometimes went after the baby. So I'd get a phone call at like three in the morning, and Bri be all crying, begging me to come quick and pick up Chanelle, and then I hear Marcus in the background, crashing things against the wall. It a mess.

So that went on for maybe a year—Brianna's phone calls, I mean. The entire time, I used to tell her how she could do better than Marcus, but it wasn't no good. Which just go to show why love such a powerful thing. It like a drug. You know what I'm saying? It get hold of you, and then, suddenly, you ain't thinking right. I mean, Bri *fine*. She could've done a damn sight better than a thug ass wannabe like Marcus.

So now it like a year later, and by now I don't even answer the phone no more if I know it Bri. But then she cross me up one afternoon, call me up at a decent hour, and she in a panic—which worry me 'cause it a different kind of panic from when Marcus beating on her. It take me about five minutes to get her calmed down enough to figure out what going on.

Well, to make a long story short, now she got Child Welfare on her case. It turn out Marcus go to town on the two of them, Bri and Chanelle, a week before—and then one of the white ladies at Chanelle's day care stuck in her nose and filed a report. So now Brianna bawling into the phone, saying how Child Welfare going to come 'round tomorrow, how they going to ask questions, how they going to find bruises. Then she bawling even louder, saying how she can't lose Chanelle, how if she lose Chanelle she kill herself.

That when I get an idea.

I tell her I'll bring Janine by in the morning—Janine, that my niece. She only a month and a half older than Chanelle, so it like the two of them could be twin sisters.

But Bri still don't get it. "Why I need Janine over here?"

So I tell Bri that she can pretend like Janine is Chanelle, and meanwhile, I'll take Chanelle home with me until Child Welfare gone.

"You think we get away with it?"

"They just babies," I tell her. "Who going to know?"

So that what happened.

I waited till Vanessa—that my big sister—left for work the next morning, and then I snuck the baby out the house. I even swiped a couple extra Pampers, 'cause with Bri you don't know what she got and what she don't got. Then I drove up to Bri's place and switch Janine for Chanelle. I'm a little worried, you know, but not too much 'cause I'm pretty sure it going to work. Child Welfare mostly white people, and, well, I figure white people ain't going to know one black baby from another.

Bri grab me by the hand as I'm carrying Chanelle out the door. It her way of thanking me without saying the words. You know what I'm saying? It like a black thing. Sometime, words ain't good enough, so you grab somebody by the hand and squeeze.

I just smile back at her. "It ain't no *thing.*"

Then I head downstairs with Chanelle.

Well, I was planning to bring her home with me, but it a nice morning, so I figure I'll take her to the park. Except once we get there, I start to notice how she different from the last time I minded her. Before, she just like a normal baby. But now she don't want to do nothing. Just lay quiet and still, like a sack of flour. If it Janine, she been squirming and fussing, trying to get loose and explore. Granted, Chanelle six weeks younger. Fifteen months old. But I swear I ain't never held a baby so uninterested in stuff. Even that thing babies do—you know, that trick when their hands close up 'round your finger—even *that* don't interest her. I'm poking my finger right in the palm of her hands, and I don't get nothing back.

But I don't pay it too much mind 'cause, like I said, I got me a nice morning, and I ain't got nothing to accomplish except sit in the park and kill time. Which is what I do. Meanwhile, time passes. Get near lunch, and I'm thinking I should give Bri a call, you know, find out if Child Welfare's even got there yet. But first I figure I'll do the diaper thing. But, then, as I'm changing the baby, I start noticing stuff. Like, for example, the second I go for the snaps on her diaper, Chanelle tense up—like she having a seizure or some such thing. I mean, it like her entire body tighten up like a fist. Kind of spooky. First, she tighten up; then, she start to shake. So I'm thinking maybe it *is* a seizure. But then, a second later, she go limp. Just like she was before, like nothing going on.

Well, I get the diaper off, and that when I see the burns. That poor child got cigarette burns on her thighs, right up near her privates! Made me cry just to look at 'em! But about one second later I know what I got to do. . . .

I got to get Janine out of there!

So I quick do the diaper thing, and then I'm like running back to Bri's place, and that poor child like a sack of flour again, and I'm huffing and puffing, and I'm running till I can't run no more.

Then, just as I get to Bri's apartment building, I see a white man and a white lady walking out the front door. Which I know is the people from Child Welfare. I walk past them real slow—you know, real cool. Like nothing going on. But then the white lady, she maybe twenty-five years old, one of these types that looks at black people and auto-matically smiles—you know the type, like she still be smiling even if she getting shook down—she stop all of a sudden as I'm walking past. Yo, I felt like my heart going to come right out my mouth! But I'm still cool on the outside, smiling back at her, and then she poke her finger at me—and then I realize she want to look at Chanelle. Not 'cause she suspicious, but only 'cause it a baby, and she want to go *googly-googly* at it.

So now I got that white lady, and now, a second later, I got that white man too—I got both of them poking at Chanelle with their fingers, going *googly-googly*. Well, I'm just about dying on the inside, my heart going a mile a minute; I figure they bound to notice how Chanelle don't move, how she just lay still like a sack of flour, and then they going to get suspicious. Except then, out of nowhere, just as the two of 'em start poking her, Chanelle perk up. She grinning wide, doing that squeeze trick 'round their fingers.

Then the white lady look up at me.

"What a beautiful baby!"

"Thank you," I say, still playing cool.

"What's her name?"

"Janine."

Then the white man say, "Do you live nearby?"

"Not too far," I say.

"Does your baby play with other children in the neighborhood?"

I kind of squint at him. "She too young to play much, mister."

Then it the white lady's turn. "Do you know a woman named Brianna Thorpe?"

"I know her some," I say.

"Do you know her baby?"

"I know she got one."

"Do you know the baby's name?"

"I think it Chanelle."

"Does Chanelle seem . . . well, does she seem a normal, happy baby?"

"Can't tell for sure," I say. "Seem okay to me though."

Then it back to the white man. "Do you think Brianna Thorpe is a responsible parent?"

"She a mother," I say. "Who to say if she responsible or not?"

Then it the lady again. "We're not here to judge. We only want to be sure Chanelle's all right."

"Then why you ask me? Seem like you should be asking Brianna."

The lady smiling again. "Thank you for your time, Miss . . ."

"You very welcome," I say.

Then I turn around and walk on into the building.

Brianna buzz me in a second later, and I run up the side stairs. She meet me at the door, and then the two of us rush back inside her apartment and watch from the corner of her window until the man and woman drive off. Then I turn to her and say, "Girl, you got to get your shit together!"

She just look at me hopeless. "I'm trying Keisha. Lord know, I'm trying."

"Then try harder," I say. "You got to look after your child!"

Now she start sobbing. "I know I do. I know I do."

"If you know it, then do it. Straight up, Bri. You got to get out. I'm being for real. If not for your own sake, then for Chanelle's. 'Cause the children, they the future. You know what I'm saying?"

"I know you right," she say. "But it so hard. I love him so much. It make me hurt inside just to think about not being with him."

"Then you got to be strong. Remember, the children is our future. Don't you ever forget that."

"But I love him so much, Keisha. So much it impossible. He give me what I need. You know what I'm saying?"

"Well, another man give you that too. That, and more besides maybe."

Then she look at me kind of sly. "You still being with Africa?"

"Africa!" I say. "What he got to do with the situation?"

"I always like Africa. He a good man. You still being with him?"

"Yes, I'm still being with him!"

"I just asking, Keish," Bri say. "I just want to know what's what."

"Well," I say, "now you know."

For a second, we just kind of stare out the window.

Then I step back from the window and set down Chanelle in the crib next to Janine. The two of them just laying there, side by side, like two baby dolls. Look so much alike, they *could* be sisters. But I don't let myself get too distracted. I still want to get Janine out of there—just in case Marcus show up unexpected. I mean, what kind of man do what he did to a baby?

But then, on the train ride home, I start to think *why* he did what he did. I'm riding with Janine asleep on my lap, safe and sound, and, suddenly, I'm wondering what make Marcus the way he is? He a thug ass, true, but maybe that what being a black man in America do to you. You know what I'm saying? The reason a black man beat on his woman or child is maybe because he facing racism every day of his life. On the job. In the streets. Everywhere a black man go, there go racism to beat him back down. Maybe it just get to a point where he feel like he got to beat something back—you know, to keep from going out his mind. You know what I'm saying?

Now, I forget, what got me started talking about Marcus?

Oh yeah, I remember.

What I was saying was how when you don't respect yourself, it wind up messing with your mind. I know that personally 'cause of what happened next. I get a phone call about six months after the thing with Brianna and Chanelle—Mona Lisa calling me, crying hysterical into the phone, asking me if I heard the news. So I ask her what news, and she tell me the news on Channel 11. Now she just yelling in the phone, *Turn on the t.v.! Turn on the t.v.!*

So I turn on the t.v.

The first thing I see is cops shoving Marcus into a squad car. I get a bad feeling right away in my guts. 'Cause it lots of cops, detectives too. Plus, reporters. Cameras going off, *pop, pop, pop.*

So I think: *That motherfucker gone and killed Brianna!*

But then, the next thing, Bri come stumbling out onto the sidewalk, in front of her apartment, talking to a reporter. Except she ain't talking, just crying hysterical like usual. So now I got Brianna crying hysterical on the television, and I got Mona Lisa crying hysterical in the phone, and I still don't know what the hell going on.

Then it finally come to me: *Marcus gone and killed the baby.*

That the worst moment of my life. I felt like *I* killed Chanelle. Right off, I drop down onto my knees and ask God almighty please forgive me. But it ain't no good, 'cause I know I ain't going to never forgive myself. So then I go running into the bedroom and snatch Janine right out her playpen, and I start hugging her and kissing her and squeezing her real tight—almost frighten that poor child to death. But can't help myself; I keep thinking how it could've been her, how much she and Chanelle look alike that time in the crib.

It make me want to cry even now.

You got a tissue?

I know it been five years, but it still so sad to remember about it. Maybe if I don't think to switch the two babies, maybe Chanelle still be alive right now. You know what I'm saying? For months afterwards, I think it all on me. I think I killed Chanelle just as much as Marcus did. I lay in bed for weeks just thinking about it. It such a tragedy. I lost nine pounds, I got the shakes and fever. I think about it and think about it until it all thought out.

But I didn't get no answers.

That was when I lost my self-respect. I finally crawled out of bed—except it wasn't me no more. I was like the worst slut ho for a year afterwards. There wasn't nothing or no one I wouldn't do. Like I was punishing myself. You know what I'm saying? Like if I got down on my knees often enough, maybe God take notice and forgive me.

Then one night Africa set me straight. I was out in an alley behind a club in Crooklyn, getting ready to do Lord knows what to Lord knows who. Truthfully, I don't even remember who I was with that night. All I remember is Africa grabbing me by the right arm and dragging me away. And when I say dragging, I do mean *dragging*. Dragging me right back through the club, then back outside onto the sidewalk—I'm talking *on my butt!* And guess what I'm doing the entire time he dragging me. Laughing. I was so fucked up out of my mind, yo, I was laughing and laughing! I mean, Africa about yanking my right arm clear out its socket—and I'm crazy mad laughing!

That when he slap me real hard across the face.

Then he look me in the eye and say, "Yo!"

"What up?"

I start giggling again, and he slap me again hard.

"Damn, nigga!" I say.

"I don't know what the hell got into your brain, Keisha, but you one fucked up bitch!"

Now suddenly I'm bawling my eyes out, right there on the sidewalk. "I want to die, Africa. I'm being for real. I want to die."

"Why you want to die?"

So then I tell him the whole story, about how I helped Brianna trick Child Welfare, about how I found the burns on the baby's thighs—I tell him the whole shameful thing.

Afterward, Africa shaking his head. "It's a straight up tragedy. Ain't no way around it."

"It all my fault."

"How you figure that?"

"I just told you!" I say. "I switched the babies. It my idea."

"True, but it's Brianna's baby you switched with. If anyone, it's all on her."

"But she would've never thought it herself. You know what I'm saying?"

Then Africa, he stop and think. "When you get right down to it, you know who it's all on?"

"Who?"

"America is who!"

"How you figure that?"

"Well, just think about it," he say. "The only reason you did what you did is 'cause you knew Brianna wasn't going to get no fair shake from Child Welfare—'cause she's black, I mean."

"Lord know it the truth."

"So you wouldn't have did what you did if it wasn't for racism! That's what I'm saying."

Which is true.

See, it took me realizing racism was to blame before I could get right with myself again. It a tragedy, a child dying like that. But ain't no one to blame except racism. If it wasn't for racism, Marcus wouldn't never have gotten like how he was. And if it wasn't for racism, Brianna wouldn't never been buggin' about Child Welfare taking away Chanelle. And as for me, myself—well, I was only trying to do for a homegirl. You know what I'm saying?

Ain't no one to blame but racism.

Yo, I'll always love Africa 'cause he the one who set me straight. Which is why he my honey nigga.

WELL, WHAT DO YOU THINK ABOUT MY GIRL LAKEISHA? She's a natural born trip, ain't she?

She said she talked till you ran out of tape. That's the thing about females. They get wound up, ain't no off switch. You know what I'm saying? You could ask 'em a polite *What up?* and get their life stories. You get the four-one-one . . . plus the star-six-nine, plus the area code, plus the caller I.D.

By the way, Keisha wouldn't tell me what she talked about, so I guess that's between her and you. Hey, that's cool. Truthfully, I know the bitch *believes* what she say. I mean, she's got her own bitch reality, and that's how it should be. All I'm saying is there's bitch reality, and then there's *real* reality. You know what I'm saying? Bitches just see the world totally different, you know, like they looking at it through their pussies instead of their eyes.

But that's like, how they say, besides the point. 'Cause I got something to show you. . . .

Fool, I *know* you can't read it yet! I just had the work done this morning. It says *I'M 'BOUT IT, 'BOUT IT.* I thought I needed a piece to go with the left arm—you know, where it says *149 FOR LIFE.* It's like the two of 'em together, the two pieces, that's what I'm all about. It's like my life story.

What does it mean? What do you think it means?

Well, it means the words: *I'm 'bout it, 'bout it.* Yo, like *I'm 'bout it.* Except double. Like there ain't no doubt whatsoever—*I'm 'bout it, 'bout it.* So I'm *'bout it, 'bout it.*

No *doubt!*

What?

Why? Do I *seem* like I'm in a good mood?

Then I suppose I must be in a good mood!

Now, the question that's on your mind is: Why would a no good nigga such as myself be in a good mood on a Wednesday afternoon? Do you think it's 'cause I slam-dunked a damn basketball? Is that what it takes to make a nigga smile? Then what do you suppose—as a Caucasian person, I mean—what do you suppose could put a grin on a crazy nigga's face in the middle of the week? Well, let me give you three hints:

Pussy.

Pussy.

And . . .

Pussy.

You give up?

Now the reason I said three hints is 'cause there's three of 'em. Pussies, I'm talking. That's right. Yeah, I had two lots of times, but I ain't never even *thought* to have three at once. To be truthful, yo, I don't even know how that works—three at once, I mean. I don't know what gets stuck where. But Herc says he once had three at once, so I figure I got to go for it. You know what I'm saying? Now here's the kicker:

It's three chinks.

Molly, Sally, and Liang.

College bitches, too. Smart. But not in a glasses kind of way. They go to an art school somewhere downtown—I forget the name. Some kind of *Institute.* I met 'em at a party at a club; I got invited 'cause the host is a regular customer of mine. Right off, I know Molly and Sally are freaks. They got that whole chink-ho thing going on—you know, standing in the corner of the room, checking me out, then looking down real quick, like "So sorry." Then, as soon as I ain't paying 'em no more attention, checking me out again.

So, finally, I walk right up to 'em. I mean, I get right up in their faces, look 'em right in their slitty eyes. Ain't no way they're going to pretend no more 'cause I'm right there.

And I'm like, "Ay yo trip!"

Molly looks up first. She's got a real chink face. Round as a dime. She got the slit eyes, the flat nose. Got no meat on her bones. No titties. No booty. She's a chink, though, so you got to accept that. But the thing that got me was the hair. So black it's like a mirror. Like if the light was shining just right you could almost check yourself out in her hair. Plus, *long* ain't even the word. It ran straight down to her butt crack.

Now Sally's a different sort of chink. Not as round-faced, more like a kitty-cat. Plus, she's got that glowy blue stuff around her eyes. What I liked about Sally was her belly. It was peeking out, a couple of inches of skin, between her shirt and her jeans. Personally, I always liked chink bellies. The skin's dark and smooth, and you know chinks don't get too hairy. So they can wear their jeans real low, like to where the average female would show the edge of the forest.

Well, I walk over to them, like I said, and now the two of 'em just kind of smiling together.

"I notice the two of you been checking me out," I say. "Well, you like what you looking at?"

"You're a very good dancer," Molly says to me.

Then it's Sally's turn. "We like how you dance."

"Now that *ain't* the truth," I shoot back. "'Cause I don't dance worth a rat's ass. The truth is you into me. Both of you. Ain't no use denying it 'cause I got radar."

They start giggling.

"What?" I say. "You don't believe I got radar?"

More giggling.

So I start beeping, going *beep beep beep,* swiveling my hips back and forth, you know, like I got radar—except it's dick radar. That gets 'em going; they bagging up, laughing like I'm Eddie and Martin rolled in one, and meanwhile, I'm swiveling and beeping, swiveling and beeping. I don't stop till I'm wedged in between 'em. So now I pull 'em tight around me. Got my palms flat on their asses, and I can feel their yellow cunts getting hotter and wetter through their jeans. Yo, it ain't even a minute from the time I walked

80

over, but the two 'em already into me like nobody's business.

That's when Liang shows up.

Soon as she comes over, I'm like: Dag, I *got* to get me some of that. I mean, Liang is *fine*. You know what I'm saying? Not fine just for a chink. I mean, straight up *booyaa*. I don't know how to describe her, exactly. Like a model, I guess. Tall, maybe six feet. Got the highest pair of titties I ever seen. Not just high but round, I mean like *mad* round. Perfect round. Not small neither. She's got on a white tee-shirt with no sleeves, and she's got these mad round titties with no bra underneath, and I'm thinking maybe she's got fake titties—that's how good her titties look. But I don't think the titties were fake. I don't know why. It's like how she carried herself, like she wouldn't bother with fake titties or fake contacts or fake nothing.

The second I laid eyes on Liang, it's like Molly and Sally don't matter to me no more. Except they do matter 'cause they're with Liang. That's when I know I got to get with the three of 'em at once. You know what I'm saying? I got to get next to Molly and Sally and then hope Liang joins it. 'Cause Liang—she don't want no part of me. That much I know just from the look on her face. I think she's prejudice against black men. It's *that* look. You know? It's like her eyes are already saying: *I ain't going to get with no monkey nigga!*

Yo, I *hate* chinks like that!

But still, I can't take nothing from her. She's got it going on, and damned if she don't know it.

So she struts on over to the three of us, looks me up and down—just kind of dissing me with her eyes. Then she tugs hard on Molly's sleeve and says out loud, "Now we go?"

Molly glances at me, then past me towards Sally.

Sally just shrugs—like she don't want to go, but it's up to Molly and Liang.

Then Molly turns back to Liang. "Maybe soon."

Liang just stares at her, half angry and half sarcastic.

That's when Liang looks me right in the eyes. "They good girls. You not get sex tonight."

Soon as Sally hears what Liang said, she starts giggling again. But nervous, not like she thinks it's funny. Molly's just cringing meanwhile—like she want to be somewhere else 'cause she knows what's about to happen. Like it's a nightmare she had before.

Then Liang jabs her finger in my chest. "Why you not find black girls have sex with?"

So I'm like, "You better watch your mouth, bitch."

"Or what?" she says. "You hit a woman? No real man hit a woman."

"What you know about a *real* man? You ever in your entire life been with one?"

"You not get sex. Leave us alone."

"Yeah, well, fuck you!"

"You ugly besides," she says.

Now for some reason, that just cracks me up. Maybe 'cause of how she said it—like it came out of nowhere. So I'm cracking up right in her face, and every time I glance up, Liang's still glaring at me, still got her eyebrows riding down low over her eyes. But then, like a miracle, she starts cracking up too! It's like she caved in, like she held that mean look on her face as long as she could, and then she couldn't hold it no more.

She laughs for maybe a half minute, non-stop. Then she just smiles at me.

"You still not get sex!"

But that cracks her up again.

"That suits me 'cause I wouldn't bone your nasty ass in the first place."

After that, we dance for maybe a half hour. Not Liang. She just watches me dance with Molly and Sally. I ain't danced so much since . . . since never, I don't think. But every so often, I glance over my shoulder, and I notice

Liang's checking me out. Not in a black way—not like how Lakeisha would do it. But sweet. Sweet and foxy at the same time. You know what I'm saying? Like she's into me, but she's fighting it hard.

Finally, she walks out onto the dance floor. Not to dance, just to tell Molly it's time to roll. Then Molly taps Sally on the shoulder, and then Sally turns to me and just kind of shrugs.

I shrug back, like: *Whatever!*

Then Sally gives me a kiss on the right cheek, and then Molly gives me a kiss on the left cheek. Then I stare at Liang.

She smiles real sugar at me for a second, then turns and rolls straight out the door. Molly and Sally follow her, and next thing I know, I'm standing alone on the dance floor.

And I'm like, *Damn!*

But then, about a minute later, Sally rushes back into the club. Rushes right up to me—I ain't moved from the dance floor—and kisses me again. Except now it's on the mouth, and she even slips me a half second of tongue. Then she hands me a folded up piece of paper; then, a second later, she's back out the door. I just stand there, stupid—I *still* ain't moved from the dance floor. Finally, I just shake my head and slide on over to the bar where it's light enough to read. So I unfold the paper—and guess what's written down. Sally's phone number. And right underneath Sally's number is Molly's number.

And right underneath Molly's is Liang's!

I mean, like, *bitches.* Go and figure 'em!

What?

No, I ain't called 'em just yet. You got to play the game. You know what I'm saying? If I was just out to bag Molly and Sally, I'd have closed the deal the next night. But Liang, she's different.

How?

Well, just different. It's kind of hard to explain—especially, no offense, to a white person. The thing is . . . I don't even know if it's going to make sense to you. It's like, to get with the average female, you got to show her how bad you want it. Spike had it right. It's that *Please baby please baby please baby please.* That's how you get next to Molly and Sally. But with Liang, it's like backwards of that. With a female like Liang, you got to show her how little you want it, how it don't make no difference if you get it or not. You got to make her feel like she's just another sniff of tuna. Just tuna on a stick. You know what I'm saying?

So the first rule is you don't call.

Dig: You tell your *dawg* to call!

Here's how it's going to go down: I'm going to call Molly and Sally myself, tomorrow, and then wait three days. That should give Molly and Sally enough time to tell Liang they got their calls—and enough time for her to expect hers. Then I'm going to get Eddy to call her. It's going to seem like I'm passing her off to him, like I ain't interested in her for myself. Mess with her brain waves. You know what I'm saying? Hurt her feelings. Get her standing in front of a mirror trying to figure out what's wrong.

That's what you do with filet mignon. You got to tenderize it before you put it on the grill.

YO, TONIGHT'S THE *NIGHT!* YOU KNOW WHAT I'M SAYING?
The night of the black wolf . . . *aaahhhooo!*
In effect!
Africa's going to break himself off a little sumpin' sumpin'. Going to drop a drop of motion in the ocean. Going to do it up, do it down, do it every which way around!
In effect!
You know what I'm saying?
What? In effect?
It's like, you know, *phase one.* I got Molly and Sally lined up for tonight. So that's the start of phase one. Now here's how it's going to go down. I'll get with one of 'em tonight—probably Sally 'cause she's the freakier of the two. I figured that out over the phone. It's in the way she giggles all the time. Like, for instance, when I said, "You ain't never got with a nigga, have you?" She don't answer, just giggles. It's that chinky giggle too. Like as if she's saying: *So sorry, me never thought such a thing!*

But I think, deep down, chink bitches are mostly freaks. It's just they're kind of schooled to keep it inside. You know what I'm saying? It's like, in their culture, bitches are trained to be scared of dick. Except that just makes 'em want it more. I seen a porno once where a chink got it three ways at once. Down the throat. Up the ass. And in the twat. Yo, that had to hurt! Except that freaky chink was loving it! She was even doing two more with her hands!

But I got sidetracked.

So, yeah, I'll likely do Sally tonight. But yet, at the same time, I might wind up doing both of 'em. It depends on Molly. That's what I predict. But even if I do get with both of 'em, it don't mean nothing. Just part of phase one. Phase *two,* now *that's* what I'm talking about! That's maybe a week or two down the road, when I get Liang to join in. I predict that's what she'll do, too. Not even so much 'cause she wants to—yo, I still think she's prejudiced. But likely she'll join in just to figure out why I ain't interested in her.

Remember like I was saying last time? About how I'm going to mess with their minds? Now you know what I meant. You got to *strategize* to get with females—be they chinks or what have you.

So . . . how come we always talking about me?

Yeah, I know, I know. It ain't about the two of us; it's about getting the truth out. Well, I'm down with that. I'm, you know, 'bout it, 'bout it. Speaking the truth to power, I mean. Raising awareness. Except all I'm saying is how come we don't never talk about *you?* Like people do, I mean. Just out of being polite. Take for an example, soon as I sit down, how come I don't never get to ask, like, *What up?* It ain't only a black thing, you know. It's a people thing. Manners and such. Dag, I don't even know where you was from!

That's right, I'm asking: *Where was you from?*

No shit!

Yo, I'm from Bayside. So it's almost like we was neighbors. Where you go to school? No, not college! I'm talking *school.* Like, where you hang? Cardozo? *No shit!* I used to do Little League on that field. Third-fucking-base, man, check it out!

Man, I *sucked* at baseball!

I don't want to sound racist, but baseball ain't no game for a black man. It ain't got no pump to it, you know, no beat. You know what I'm saying? Just a lot of standing around, waiting. Pondering. Pondering, that's a white thing. Naturally, you got your exceptions—you got your Griff's, your Straw's, your Barry B's. But when I was doing Little League, I just felt wrong. You know what I'm saying? Like *wrong.* Like I couldn't *not* think about shit. I mean, I'd look down and notice what my feet were doing. What direction they were pointing. Then I'd start to feel what my toes were doing inside my cleats. How they were bent up. Sure enough, that's when the ball would get hit at me.

I was lucky I didn't get killed!

Now I remember this red-haired kid who played right field. His name was Billy, I think. Maybe William, but we called him Billy. Red hair and freckles, the works. Real skinny. I'm talking *mad* skinny. Like you could see his ribs when hc took a breath. It don't matter. But the thing about Billy was how he put his heart in it. He couldn't play for shit, even worse than me. But he used to go after balls like I don't know what. He'd go diving into the stickerbush after a foul ball. I mean, it's a damn *foul ball!* People be yelling at him, *Look out, Billy! Look out!* But in he'd go, head first, diving right into that stickerbush like it was cheerleader twat. You know what the kicker is? He never caught the damn ball. Not once. He'd go diving in, and then we'd have to run and drag him back out. Damn, he'd be scratched up! His nose. His lips. His eyelids. Stickers in his hair. Stickers down his pants.

For a damn *foul ball!*

I even said it to him after about the third time, "Yo, Billy, why you always go diving in the stickerbush?"

He kind of stares at me confused. His lower lip's scratched up and now it's drooping down, and you almost could see the wheels turning inside his head, like the question ain't never occurred to him. Then, finally, he looks at me and starts to smile. "I thought I had it."

"You thought you had it?"

"I thought I had it."

"But you ain't never had it, Billy. You ain't never going to have it neither."

Now he's got that confused stare again. "How do you know?"

"I *know,* Billy. You ain't never going to have it. It ain't going to happen. I'm telling you straight up for real, man."

Then, suddenly, the wheels start turning again. The two of us sitting on the end of the bench, and I'm watching the wheels turning inside Billy's head, and I'm thinking maybe I'm getting through to him, maybe it's starting to penetrate that he ain't never going to catch a ball diving into that stickerbush. Then, finally, he gets it. I swear, you could see him get it; the exact second he got it, you could see it in his eyes! Except then, out of nowhere, he gets a hurt look on his face. Like now he's got it, and he wished he didn't.

Then he just gets up and walks to the other end of the bench. He don't say a word. Don't look at me. Don't get mad. Don't get nothing. Just walks away like he's got more figuring out to do.

Meanwhile, I'm feeling sorry for the motherfucker, but, yo, I'm thinking he's better off knowing the truth.

Well, it's like three innings later, and another ball's hit down the line, and I turn around to see what Billy's going to do. He just stands there for about half a second—and I'm thinking maybe I got through to him. He's just standing there, with the wheels in his head turning, and then, all of a sudden, he tears out after that ball. I mean, I ain't never seen no white boy run like that. He just *tears out.* So he's tearing out, and he's running, and his arms are waving and flailing—you know, the way white boys run. So he's running and running, and now here comes the stickerbush, and I can't bear to look, so I shut my eyes . . . except then I open 'em again 'cause I got to know what happens. It's like a slasher flick. You know what I'm saying? Well, to make a long story short, Billy goes flying into that stickerbush harder than he ever did before, and of course the ball lands about fifteen feet in front of him. I mean, the motherfucker had no chance at that ball! So the rest of us go trotting over, like usual, and, like usual, we about to drag him out again, but the second we move him, he starts moaning and groaning. Turns out he busted his left arm!

For a damn foul ball!

Yo, there ain't nothing on God's green earth dumber than a red-haired white boy!

So you from Bayside, huh? You know a bitch called Celeste?

What?

No, I don't know her last name! How many black girls called Celeste you think ever lived in Bayside? I was just wondering 'cause I got with her once on the practice field at Cardozo.

What?

No, it ain't like that. The only reason I even bring up Celeste is 'cause I thought you'd want to hear about what happened. Not even about the fucking—shit, I already told you enough about that. The thing about Celeste, the thing that makes her stand out, is it's the only time I ever unprided myself to get with a bitch. It's the only time, and if I had to do it over again, I wouldn't do it. I was just a kid. Like maybe fourteen. I'd fucked a few bitches, but I still didn't know shit. Yo, I was a real whippersnapper. Thought I knew it all, but I didn't know *shit*. All I knew was I was into pussy. Couldn't get enough of it. That's the black man's affliction, if you get right down to it. That's the reason he ever let the white man get on top. 'Cause the black man was too busy chasing pussy to watch his back. Now don't get me wrong. The white man like his pussy too. But not like how the black man like pussy. The black man—he don't just like pussy. He *love* pussy.

You know what I'm saying?

So I was looking to get with Celeste 'cause she was fine—except it didn't much matter if she was fine 'cause I was fourteen, and I was into pussy. Celeste knew it too. She was a year older, and she knew I was into pussy, and she played me good. Made me take her out to a movie twice before I even got to feel her up. But the third time, I knew I was going to get some. It was a Saturday night, and the first two times was on a Tuesday or some shit like that. And when you're fourteen, Saturday night means pussy. It's like an unwritten rule. But yet Celeste still wanted me to meet her father before I took her out that night.

Well, I caught the bus to her house. That right there tells you how stupid I was; it was an extra fare; I should've just met her at the movies, like I did before, but, like I said, she said her old man wanted to meet me. So I did like I was told. I hopped the Q17 to her house—even though ten minutes later me and Celeste was going to have to get right back on the bus to go to the movie, and then afterwards catch another bus to get to the Cardozo practice field. That was the place where the junior high niggas used to take their dates to fuck.

So I walk up the path to Celeste's house. It's a nice flat kind of house with a lot of red bricks and stones. That's a real white people's neighborhood by the way—Bayside. Her daddy's waiting inside the door. Big old black man. Maybe six foot two. Maybe forty-five years old. He told me Celeste was in the bathroom and she'd be out in a couple of minutes. Then he sat me down on the couch, and he parked his big old black ass next to me. Right off, it felt wrong. Like a detective sweating a perp. For like ten seconds, he just looked me up and down. Didn't say nothing. Finally, he asked me if I wanted a glass of *pop*.

Yo, I had to think for a second to realize he meant soda. I nodded my head. "Yeah."

I didn't want no soda, but I didn't want him looking me up and down no more.

He stood up real slow and then walked real slow to the kitchen. I half-wanted to bounce, you know, roll on out of there and hop the Q17 back home—I was thinking pussy ain't worth what I'm going through. But then, when I thought about it, I decided it was.

Meanwhile, Celeste's old man came back with a glass of soda. *Dag,* I can even remember what the glass looked like. It was a big old Disney glass, the kind my old man used to get at gas stations whenever he filled up. So I take it from him and start drinking. Not that I'm thirsty. I just figure if I'm drinking, I don't got to talk.

He watches me drink.

When I'm maybe half way done, he says, "You don't talk too much, do you Kevin?"

I shake my head no, don't talk.

"You nervous?"

I do it again—shake my head.

"I would understand if you were nervous."

I set down the glass. "I ain't nervous."

He smiles at me. "Celeste tells me you make good grades."

"Sometimes," I say. "But it ain't like that."

"Are you saying my daughter lied to me?"

"I ain't saying that. I ain't saying nothing."

"Well, do you or don't you make good grades?"

"It's like I said. *Sometimes.* Sometimes I do. Sometimes I don't. What I'm saying is it ain't like that."

He don't like that answer. He tilts his head kind of sarcastic at me. "Do you *try* to make good grades, Kevin?"

"Why should I? It don't mean nothing."

"Good grades get you into college," he says.

"College don't mean nothing neither."

"What does your father do for a living?"

"Teaches."

He smiles even bigger. "Your father's a teacher?"

"That's right."

"But you think college don't mean nothing?"

"That's what I said. It don't mean nothing."

"You think your father would agree with you?"

"Don't know. Why don't you ask him yourself?"

"Your father ever teach you to respect your elders?"

"Why should I?"

He smiles so big I think his face is going to blow up. "Well, Kevin, I could give you a lot of reasons. I could tell you how it says to respect your elders in the Bible. I could tell you how your elders cared for you when you were too small to care for yourself. I could even tell you how human

91

society depends on youngsters giving respect to their elders. But instead I'd like to put it in more direct terms. Do you mind if I do that, Kevin?"

"Whatever."

He slides in real close to me, puts his arm over my shoulder. "The main reason you should respect your elders, and I say this in all sincerity, is they just might beat the living daylights out of you if you don't."

I look up at him. He's still smiling.

"Do you understand what I'm saying, Kevin?"

I nod and smile back at him. "I understand."

But what I'm thinking right then is: *Do you understand I'm going to fuck your daughter's pussy tonight?*

"Good," he says. "I like to be understood."

That's when Celeste comes out of the bathroom. Her old man turns around, like nothing's going on, like he ain't said what he just said, and he jumps up from the couch as she's walking through the living room; then he puts out his hand, like it's a dance, and he twirls her 'round in her dress.

Then he turns back to me, and he's got that sarcastic look again. "Tell me the truth, Kevin. Doesn't she take your breath away?"

Celeste's all fake mad. "Stop it, Daddy. You're making me blush."

It's like the two of 'em together got an act going on, like they're playing me.

"We going to miss the flick," I say.

So the two of us scoot out the door a minute later, not a second too soon for me, and we hop the bus a minute after that. We don't talk much on the ride, not for the first couple of minutes, but then Celeste turns to me and says, "My daddy likes you, Kevin. I can tell."

That just blows me away, the fact that she don't have a clue.

"What you talking about, girl? That man, he hates my guts!"

"Why do you think that? Did he tease you? He does that sometimes when I bring a boy to the house. But the secret is, if he teased you, that just shows he likes you."

"That man hates my guts. Ain't nothing more to say. Plus, he don't even talk like a black man."

"How is a black man supposed to talk?"

"Not like that."

"Like what?"

I'm shaking my head side to side. "I don't even want to say it."

"Go on and say it, Kevin. I know what you're thinking."

"All right," I say. "*White.* Your old man talks like if he was white."

"I don't think there's a *white* way to talk. Or a *black* way."

"If you don't think so, then you just an ignorant bitch."

Suddenly, she pulls back in a real upset way. "What did you call me?"

"All I'm saying is you don't know what's going on with your old man."

"Oh, I understand exactly what you mean, Kevin. I just want to hear again what you said. I want to hear what you called me. So say it again unless you're a coward."

I should've bitch-slapped her right there. But, like I said, I was fourteen, and I didn't know shit.

"I didn't *call* you nothing," I say, "That's just how I talk. Like a black man."

She reaches up and hits the stop signal.

Now I'm about to panic. After what I gone through, first with the bus and then with her old man, I figure I *earned* pussy. I don't want to blow it before we even get to the movie.

So I did it . . . I unprided myself.

"I'm sorry, Celeste," I say, "I didn't mean nothing by it. I won't say it again."

She stares me down hard.

The bus rolls to a stop. The back doors slide open.

There's like a second when I ain't sure, but then she calls out to the driver, "It's okay, sir. I decided to keep going. Sorry for the inconvenience."

The doors snap shut, and the bus starts rolling again.

Well, basically, what happened is that for the rest of the night I kept telling her how sorry I was. Man, I was apologizing for how I walked, how I talked, how I dressed, how I ate. I was like a sorry-ing machine. If it had to do with me, I said I was sorry. I didn't even feel it after about the fifth time. It was like the word, *sorry,* it didn't mean nothing to me no more. Like it was just a sound that came out of my mouth.

The entire time, the only thing I kept thinking about was how I was going to get pussy.

Now you know what's the joke thing of it—the joke thing *and* the sad thing? By the end of the night, I didn't even want it no more. Pussy, I mean. Like I said, I got Celeste that night on the practice field at Cardozo. But it didn't mean shit to me. You know what I'm saying? All it meant was I could stop apologizing.

When I got home that night, I couldn't even look myself in the mirror.

YOU KNOW THE LESSON I LEARNED LAST WEEK? If bitches is wack, which they are, chink bitches *off the hook* wack! You know what I'm saying? It's like they on their period 24-seven! I mean, what's up with that? I'll tell you just exactly what happened. I hopped the downtown N to pick up Molly and Sally. Last Wednesday, I mean, the night after you and me talked. Well, I'm supposed to meet both of 'em downstairs in the lobby of their dorm. Except soon as I start up the path to the main door, the two of 'em, Molly and Sally, come running outside. Like they don't want me to set foot in the dorm. Like a black man ain't allowed. Which, by the way, he probably ain't—damn racist college! So right off the bat, I got a real bad feeling.

"Yo!" I say, 'cause they both wearing ratty old jeans and sweaters. "How we going out with you dressed like that?"

They don't answer but just kind of glance back and forth, nervous.

"Yo!" I say again, except louder. "Three of us going out or what?"

Finally, Molly looks me in the eye. "We cannot go out with you."

"Neither one?"

"We *cannot,*" Sally says. "You understand."

She says it like as if to say you *will* understand. Like it's a done deal. That only pisses me off more.

"Why the fuck not?"

"We cannot tell," she says.

I just stare at the two of 'em.

Then it's Sally again. "You understand."

"I understand you a couple of wack bitches. That's what I understand."

Then it's Molly's turn. "No, no, no! You understand!"

"I understand upside your head if you don't watch your mouth!"

95

That shuts 'em up real quick. They take a couple of steps backwards, start looking over their shoulders in the direction of the dorm. Like they about to tear out for the front door.

So I hold my hands up, you know, palms out, like *Don't worry. It's cool. I ain't going to hit you.*

I say, "All I want to know is the reason. Then I'm gone, okay?"

Sally looks at me, real desperate. "We cannot say. We *cannot.*"

The way she says it, I almost feel sorry for the crazy little ho.

Then it's Molly again: "You understand."

Now I just grin at her. It *is* kind of comical, the two of 'em, standing on the sidewalk in their nasty old clothes, jabbering away like the chinks they is. Being mysterious.

I say, "Whatever. I'm out."

I turn around and start walking back to the train.

"You understand!" Molly yells again. Or it could've been Sally, I ain't even sure. But I don't even look back, just keep walking. Not even mad. Just thinking to myself: *Serves me fucking right for messing with chow mein!*

That's when I look up.

Who do I see, leaning up against the stairs to the N Train?

Liang—that's who!

She don't even give me a *Yo!* Just gets right up in my face and starts yelling: "Why you not call me?"

"Dag, bitch!"

"You call Molly and Sally. You not call me. Why you not call me?"

I start shaking my head back and forth. The whole situation's got me fucked up in the brain. That, plus I got those high titties staring back at me, and I swear to God the titties is pissed off too. It's like I got Liang, plus both her titties, pissed off at me.

"Yo, I call whoever I damn well want."

"You think I'm not pretty? I'm much prettier! Why you not call?"

"What difference it makes to you? Ain't I just a no good nigga?"

"It make no difference. So I anyway want to know. You tell now!"

"I ain't telling you shit," I say.

Then I walk right past her and start down the stairs to the N Train.

A second later, the crazy bitch grabs me by the arm. "You tell now!"

I whip around like I'm about to lay her out. But she don't even blink. She's just staring me down like a mother-fucker. Like it's a dare. Like she thinks I *won't* lay her out.

Finally, I can't stand it no more. I say, "Yo, I'm hungry. You hungry?"

"First, you tell. Then, after you tell, food. Maybe, but not for sure. First, you tell."

So I stare *her* down for a couple of second. "I was saving you for last."

She looks at me like what I said don't make sense.

"I called Molly and Sally first," I say to her. "I was saving you for last."

Liang starts smiling. "That stupid. You must be stupid."

"If I'm stupid," I shoot back, "then how come you still standing here?"

She smiles even sweeter, crazy mad sweet. "Maybe stupid too."

"You up for dinner now?"

"Now dinner," she says.

So that's what we did. I took Liang to dinner at the Sizzlers.

Yo, I ain't *never* had no dinner like that. She starts in on me like the second the two of us sit down. Even before, come to think of it. She's on me 'cause I didn't hold the door for her.

"You are no manners person," she says to me. "Very immature."

"I ain't immature. You the one who don't know how to chill."

She shaking her head at me. "Immature, no manners person."

I'm taking shit off her, and we ain't even sat down yet! But the thing of it is, I don't give a rat's ass. It don't mean nothing to me 'cause it's Liang. But yet, on the other hand, *check it out*, it means much more 'cause it's Liang. I'm taking it and taking it the entire night, and I'm thinking to myself she don't mean none of it—except I know she do mean it 'cause I'm black. She ain't into me, yo, and she ain't never going to be into me. That's the bottom line. But as much as I tell myself that, I don't want to believe it. It's like as if I got one Africa sitting on my right shoulder telling me I don't got to take her shit, but yet I got another Africa sitting on my left shoulder telling me I do.

So afterwards, as we about to knock off our steaks, I put down my fork and knife and ask her straight out: "Why you hating on me all night? What I ever do to you?"

I get the stare again.

"What?"

Finally, she says, "My father dead."

"What that's got to do with me? He get whacked by a nigga?"

"You so stupid!"

"All right then. Why don't you school me? Your old man's dead. What I'm asking is what that's got to do with me?"

"In my country, my father carry sacks of rice across river eight hours day. Then he come home, sleep three hours maybe, then go back out and work cleaners. Then go straight from cleaners back to rice. Eighteen years, he work hard to move wife and daughter to United States. But still not enough. Enough to move . . . but except not enough to bribe. He beg my mother sell rings and jewelry. My mother not want to, but he beg and beg, and then she sell. She never forgive, and he know for sure she never forgive. But still he bribe, so family can come to United States. Come to United States two years ago. He work even more harder. Cleaners again, and also in Chinese restaurant. He get sick, he still work. Sicker, still work. Then die."

"What that got to do with me?"

She slams both her fists down on the table. "My father . . . he die give me United States! He die give me what you have! But do you know? Do you look at your life and be thanking? No, not thanking. Because stupid. Stupid person is what you are."

I sat quiet for a second, just to chill out, just so I wouldn't go off on her in the Sizzlers. "Bitch, you must be out your damn mind! You trying to shoot with *a black man?* Why should I be thanking nobody? My people, they were slaves. You know what that means—*slaves?* So your old man carried sacks of rice. Least he got paid. My people, they carried sacks of shit, and you know what they got? Sold down the river is what they got!"

She thinks on that for a minute.

Then she says, "Your father slave?"

"No."

"Your grandfather slave?"

"No. But—"

"Your grandfather father slave?"

"Who the fuck knows that far back?"

"So maybe your grandfather father slave," she says. "Maybe my grandfather father slave too. Slavery in Asia. Slavery in Africa. Slavery in America. Slavery all over the world in old days. But not now. Now, no slavery. Now, just you and me. I thanking to be in America. You should be thanking too."

"You only saying that 'cause you ain't black!"

"I think black people complain so much. I think black people like so much to complain."

"That's just plain ignornant. You don't even know how plain ignorant that sounds."

"Complain too much, black people," she say.

"I can't even have a conversation with you. You too ignorant to conversate with."

"Then why you want to go dinner with me? You not get sex."

"Yo, I get sex if I want," I say. "Just maybe not with you."

"Your brain in your penis is where your brain!"

"Well, you just a wacked out cunt. You know what I'm saying?"

She don't answer but looks at me strange. Not pissed off strange. More like *don't*-know-what-I'm-saying strange. Then I figure out she don't know the word—cunt, I mean. That give me enough time to think if I want to say it again, you know, *cunt,* or just let it go. I think maybe let it go. Except then, a second later, she come right back at me.

"You call me dirty word?"

"No—"

"You call me cunt. What means *cunt?*"

"What it means is . . . what it means is, you got me skitzing. That's what it means."

"I think *cunt* dirty word. You call me dirty word?"

"Like I said, you got me skitzing."

"You call me dirty word. Then I call you . . . *fuck.*"

"What?"

She grinning right in my face. "You fuck. Yes? I call you fuck."

It sound so stupid coming from her, that word, that I just smile.

She still grinning. "Fuck is what you are."

"Well, I got just one thing to say to that."

"What?"

"You right."

Suddenly, Liang just cracks up. I mean, she bagging so loud she got waiters staring at us from the kitchen. She slapping the table, banging her heels against the underside of the booth. And the thing is, the more she's laughing, the more I'm into it. I mean, I'm so into it, I'm like *ill*. The bitch just called me a fuck, and I'm like ill into it. I felt like I wanted to cry almost with being happy. You know what I'm saying? It's like I ain't never felt like that. Like at the same time she's kicking her heels under the table, she's kicking my heart. Like *pop pop pop*. And I'm staring at her, and I'm like crazy illing.

That's when I hear myself say, "Yo, I don't care if I get sex."

She stops laughing, gets all serious again. "You not get."

"What I'm saying is—it don't mean nothing. I don't care."

She looks at me suspicious.

"I ain't scamming," I say. "I ain't doing nothing. I'm just saying—"

"You think you get sex Molly and Sally?"

"I don't care about Molly and Sally. It ain't even a question with them no more."

Liang says real soft, like a confession almost, "You probably *get* sex Molly and Sally."

"Yo, I said I don't care."

"Why you not care?"

"I don't know. I just don't."

"Maybe go home now," she says.

"If that's what you want."

The thing is, soon as she said it, I realized it's what *I* wanted. To go home, I mean. What I'm saying is *I didn't want to do her.* I mean, naturally, I *wanted* to do her. Like I ain't never wanted to do no bitch before. But yet I didn't want to do her right away. It's hard to explain. It's like . . . a *concept.* I knew if I did her, that would be the end of it. She'd be did, and then that's that.

And I'll tell you what else.

I was scared.

Yo, I ain't lying. I was scared to do her. It didn't make no sense. I ain't been scared since like my third time. But I'm sitting there in the Sizzlers, staring across the table at Liang, and I realize all of a sudden I'm scared shitless at the thought of doing her.

So I throw down for dinner, 'cause it don't mean nothing to me—the money, I mean. Then afterwards it's me and Liang walking back to the dorms. Only it's like the two of us ain't even walking together. She's going on the inside of the sidewalk, next to the stores, and I'm going way out near the curb. We don't say nothing either. Just keep going. It's like dumb stupid, how we going. Together, but not together. Finally, I decide to find out if we even *is* together. So I slow up walking. Not much. Just enough so, if she don't slow up, she's going to slide a couple of steps in front.

Except she slows up.

Soon as I slow up, Liang slows up too.

So now at least I know we together. That's when I get up the nerve to say, "You ain't even thanked me yet for dinner. Didn't your mamma raise you no better than that?"

She says, like it's a pain, "Yes."

"Yes, what?"

"Yes, thank you. For dinner, I say thank you."

"You ask me, that's one weak-ass thank you."

"I say the words. I say them. I say thank you."

"You're welcome," I shoot back.

We turn onto the street where dorm's at, walk about half way up the block. Then she stops all of a sudden—like she don't want me getting too near the lobby neither. Inside the lobby, I catch sight of Molly and Sally. They peeking out from behind the front door, watching to see what happens with me and Liang. The way she looks at me, she knows I seen 'em. She glances over her shoulder and kind of grins—like Molly and Sally going to watch no matter what, so the two of us might as well get down to it.

"So what up?" I say.

"What up," she says back to me. But it don't mean nothing though. She just saying the words back to me. Like whatever's going to get said, I'm going to have to say it.

"What up with going out again? You down with that, or what?"

She squints at me. It reminds me she's a chink, the way she squints. Like she wants me to know she's got to think about it. Like she ain't made up her mind until that moment.

Finally, she says, "You call."

She don't smile or nothing.

"Maybe I call," I say. "Maybe I don't."

But I know I'm going to call, and I know *she knows* I'm going to call.

That's what starts her smiling—the fact that she *knows* I'm going to call her.

Then, she turns around and marches back into the dorm. Leaves me without even a goodnight kiss. It's like, suddenly, I'm one of them white boys I was talking about, the kind that throw down for dinner and, afterwards, wind up all grinning 'cause they got maybe a half minute of tongue. Except I ain't even white so there's no excuse. Not to mention that I didn't even get tongue.

Well, afterwards, I remember Herc's suitcasing up by Port Authority. Now me and him's got a policy. It's called the New Pussy Policy. Whenever either of us scores new pussy, he's got to let the other know first thing. Can't even shower first. That's the whole point. The pussy juice still got to be on the dick, or else it don't count. Naturally, of course, I didn't get no pussy that night. But I don't know. Seem like it's the kind of thing Herc would want to know about. What happened with Liang, I mean. So I haul ass up to Port Authority, and I find him on the corner of 40th and Eighth. It's a slow night. I can tell that right off 'cause Herc don't even got the suitcase open. He just leaning up against van parked on the corner, just staring up Eighth Avenue.

"Yo!"

He turns around. "Yo."

"What up?"

He exhales real sad, but then he perks up. "You do 'em both?"

"Who?"

"The chinks. You do 'em both?"

"Nah," I say.

"Which one you do? No, wait, don't say it. *Lilly.* Am I right?"

"Ain't no *Lilly.* It's Molly and Sally."

Herc smiles. "What difference it makes? Still two chinks. So?"

"Didn't do neither of them," I say.

He starts laughing. "And you come up here to tell me *that?*"

"I was with Liang."

"The fine one?"

"Yeah," I say.

"You fuck her?"

"Nah."

"Little suckie?"

"It ain't like that."

"No suckie, no fuckie?"

"C'mon, Herc!"

"Did you wax the ho or not?"

"That's what I'm trying to say. I didn't *want* to wax her. It ain't like that."

He thinks on what I said for a couple of seconds. Then, like for no reason, he hands me the suitcase. I don't take it at first; I don't know why he's handing it to me. But then—what the hell?—I take it. Soon as I got both hands on it, *pop,* he goes upside my head with his right hand. He ain't trying to hurt me or nothing. But he's pissed.

I take a step back; I still got hold of the suitcase though. I say, *"Damn,* nigga!"

Now he smiling again. "Okay, give me back my case."

I hand it back to him. "Why you do that?"

"Why you *think* I do that?"

"If I knew, I wouldn't ask why."

"But why you *think?*"

"Probably, 'cause I didn't get no pussy from Liang."

"Well," he say, "you didn't, did you?"

"Like I said—it ain't like that."

He put out the suitcase again. "Hold that a minute."

I step back. "I ain't going to hold that."

"All right, then look me in the eye. 'Cause I'm only going to break this down for you once. You say, 'It ain't like that.' But *it always like that.* Do you know what I'm saying? *Always.*"

"Who says, *always?*" I ask. "Maybe it ain't with Liang. You ever been with Liang?"

"I been with chinks. Lots of 'em. And it *always* like that."

"You ain't never been with Liang. So you ignorant of the situation."

"You know what you sound like? White is what you sound like."

"I don't sound no white," I say. "I'm just saying what I'm saying."

"Like a sorry ass cave boy," he say, shaking his head. "It a sad thing for me to hear."

So that's how we went on. But the thing is, Herc didn't mean it. Not none of it. He was just looking out for me, just telling me to strategize. He don't come right out with his feelings and such. Sometimes, with Herc, you got to run through what he said afterwards to pick out what he meant.

Plus, when you get right down to it, Liang *is* kind of wack. Saying one thing and meaning something mad different. It's like she's a 'nigma. You know what I'm saying? Which is just like saying she wack—except more polite.

But, yo, ain't that how it always breaks down? If a bitch is just a bitch, you know, just a hood rat, you say she's wack. But if you into her, you say she's a 'nigma.

JEROME. JEROME MILLER. That's spelled J-E-R-O-M-E, space, M-I-L-L-E-R. Africa sent me. Africa Ali. He won't be here this week. He's got what's called a "previous engagement." He didn't tell me what, not in terms of specifics. So do you want to talk to me or what?

That's good. Now . . .

Free Mumia!

Say it!

Free Mumia!

C'mon, say it!

Free Mumia!

If you don't say it, I'm not going to talk.

Free Mumia!

Dag, mister, put a little life into it. I don't care if people are staring at us. I don't give a rat's ass. It's a public restaurant. If they want to stare, that's their damn business.

Free Mumia!

That's the ticket. Now you're getting into it.

Free Mumia!

Free Mumia!

Good. Now one last time . . . you know, for Jerome.

Free Mumia!

There. Was that so difficult?

All right, now, we can get down to it. You *do* know who Mumia is, by the way. No? Then I suppose I'm going to have to darken you with knowledge—that is, if you think you can handle it. I know it sounds peculiar, doesn't it? It's kind of like a role reversal. You know, the idea that a black man would be required to educate a Caucasian. It sounds . . . what's the word? *Unnatural.* The natural order of things is for the Caucasian to educate the black man. According to the white man, that is! Just the idea that a Caucasian would need a black man to educate him—well, you know, that's just *unnatural.*

But I digress.

Mumia Abu Jamal. *Proud* black man. He was a Panther back in the sixties. That made him, right off, a threat to the powers that be. Plus, he was a journalist. Which made him a double threat. Plus, he was a Marxist. Which made him a triple threat. They *had* to take him down. So they set him up. I'm not going to bore you with the specifics. The bottom line is that he's on death row right now, rotting away in a ten foot by ten foot cell, waiting for the governor of Pennsylvania to work up the nerve to pull the switch.

Naturally, you don't believe a word I'm saying. No, there's no such thing as a political prisoner in the United States of Our Murderers—oh, excuse me, I mean the United Snakes of America. Just like you never stole the land from the red man. Just like you never raised up an empire on the backs of African slaves. Just like you never rounded up Japs into concentration camps during World War Two. None of that ever happened in America. Hell, it's not in the history books, so you *know* it can't be true.

Or can it?

Free Mumia!

Fuck them! Let them stare! Maybe next time they'll find a *whites only* restaurant.

Now the fact of the matter is, America's a damn lie. That's right. The U.S. of A. is a damn lie. It's like, you know, a *myth*—which is another way of saying it's bullshit. Don't misunderstand me. It's not the land itself that's a lie. The land is like *the land*. It's just there. But it's the *concept* of America that's a lie. We got this big concept going on about how the United States came out of Europe, the search for religious freedom and that bullshit, plus how Europe came out of so-called Ancient Greece. But it's all bullshit. The reason it's bullshit is because so-called Ancient Greece is bullshit too. The fact is, Ancient Greece isn't ancient, and it's not even Greece.

Take, for example, Socrates. I mean, when you think about Ancient Greece, who do you think about?

Socrates—am I right?

Except it's an established fact that Socrates was a black man!

That's the dirty little secret of Western Civilization. You got that painting of Socrates dying in his bathtub—and you look at that painting, and what do you see? Caucasian in a bathtub. But who painted that painting? Caucasian with a paint brush. It's like that with Jesus too. Who was also a brother incidentally. But that gets hushed up because Christianity was written down by Caucasians. Who knew that their people would never follow a black man.

Now of course Jesus was a damn lie himself. But of course that's another story.

So to speak.

You want more? I'll give you more.

Aristotle stole everything he wrote, every single thought, every single word, from the Library at Alexandria. Now the reason the Egyptians allowed him to do it is because it didn't matter to them. They figured that ideas belonged to everyone. To the people, the collective. Not to individuals. That's the reason Egyptian thinkers never even signed their shit. It just never occurred to them to claim it for their own.

So you've got Socrates. You've got Jesus. You've got Cleopatra.

Black, black, and black.

It's like a *Who's Who* of the ancient world. You know what I'm saying?

Plus, it's not only me who's saying so. University professors know the truth. I'm talking *scholarship!* You got Professor Asante at Temple. You got, of course, my man Dr. Jeffries uptown. And as for the rest of them, the Caucasian professors and their negro colleagues—even they know the truth. But most of them would lose their jobs if they ever told what they know. That's the reason you've got to go to the books. Word up! First off, there's George James's *Stolen*

Legacy. Then there's *Civilization or Barbarism* by Cheikh Anta Diop. She's from Senegal, by the way. So it's like a miracle her work even got into print. Plus, *They Came Before Columbus* by Ivan Van Sertima. I could give you like a hundred names. Hunter H. Adams. Khalil Messiha—he's the brother who discovered a working glider built by the ancient Egyptians. But the book you've just *got* to read is *Black Athena.* That tells it all. The archaeology. The myths. The cover-up by Caucasian scholars. Now here's the kicker. The absolute kicker. It was written by a Caucasian—a French guy named Bernal. Now if you got a French guy willing to speak the truth, well, need I say more?

Say what?

No, I don't mind talking about myself. I kind of expected you'd prefer to go that way. The conversation's getting a little heavy for you—I understand. Besides, the personal *is* political. Me being who I am, doing what I do, that's a political act. There's nothing more subversive for a black man to be in our society than a scholar. Every morning, as soon as I step through the gates at City College, I'm a revolutionary. Why? Because I'm contesting the status quo. You know what I'm saying?

And I've got only one reason for doing it.

To pass it on.

That's the key. It's not enough to "Learn, baby, learn" . . . you know, so you can "Earn, baby, earn." Jesse's got his rhymes, but when you get right down to it, he's only buying into the capitalist system. Any black man who does that, he's as good as Caucasian. Worse, as a matter of fact. Because the younger generation, they're going to look up to him. They're going to say, "Okay, I'm going to school to get mine—and then get out." Except you can't look at education that way. Not if you're a black man. You've got to realize you're a role model. That's the *duality* of the black man—struggling to survive as an individual and struggling to save his people at the same time. DuBois was talking about that way back in the 1800's. You know who that is, don't you? W.E.B. DuBois? I think about that every morning, as I'm walking through those gates at C.C.N.Y. It's not just me who's walking through. It's all the shorties who are going to come after me.

It's all about breaking down barriers. You know what I'm saying?

So now that I told you about myself, how about a little *reciprocation?* I mean, what's your game? Why are you so interested in Africa?

Who me?

Well, naturally, *I* think he's interesting. He's my boy. My heart. You know? Or, in the vernacular, he's my *dawg.* But what I don't quite get is why a learnéd person such as yourself, a quote-unquote *social scientist,* would be interviewing him. It's not as if Africa's well-read. I mean, let's get real. If you're after *insight,* he's not exactly the logical choice.

But that's not why you're interviewing him, am I correct? He's got it in his head that the two of you are working together, like it's a project—you know, to get the *truth* out. Again, quote-unquote. I don't believe that for a minute. So I'm sitting at home, and I'm wondering to myself what your angle might be, and I'm asking myself: "Why would someone like that be so interested in Africa?"

That's when it came to me: *Africa ain't no threat.*

What I mean by that is just that Africa's not going to tell you something you don't already know. No surprises. Nothing to upset your way of looking at things. Don't get me wrong. Like I said, he's my dawg. I wouldn't disrespect him no more than I'd disrespect Herc or Fast Eddy. Or even Lakeisha, for that matter. I'd lay it on the line for them in a second, no questions asked. I'd do hard time. Whatever it took, I'd do it. All I'm saying is . . . *let's get real.* Africa's heart's in the right place. No doubt. Hey, I even cut out articles for him to read. Lots of them, maybe two or three a

110

week. But he's just not into it. He's got a sort of general sense of what it means to be an African, but what he's lacking is, you know, *specifics.* Like what I was saying before about Socrates. Africa doesn't want to be schooled no more. I tell him education is like a lifelong project, but he doesn't want to hear about it. And don't even get me started on what he doesn't know about the Nubians. I must have lent him like five books on them, but I don't think he's read even five pages total.

I mean, he hasn't even read Angela!

You see, the thing about Africa—and it's nothing against him—it's just that he's *empirical.* What I mean by that is that he likes to think with his hands, not with his mind. Just to give an example, he's good with the kind of puzzles he can work with his hands because he doesn't have to reason them out. It's like with that colored cube. He's a damn whiz with that thing. But if you ask him how he solved it, he can't explain. That's because he doesn't *conceptualize.* You know what I'm saying? The knowledge stays in his hands. It doesn't work its way up to his mind, so it doesn't become a concept.

Now you take someone like me, on the other hand, I work with concepts. I reason things out, think them through. I link them up to other things. You know what I'm saying? I like to *delve,* you know, get at the layers underneath the layers underneath the layers. But that kind of thinking, it doesn't just happen. It's like a habit of the mind, so to speak. It's the kind of thinking you've got to train yourself to do. It takes focus. Concentration.

The situation I can relate it to is females. If I get with a female, right off, I want to know *why* I got with her. Why I got with her and not with her friend. Why she got with me and not with Africa or Fast Eddy or Herc. It's the *psychology* that interests me. People got their psychologies and their pathologies and their *what-have-you-ologies.*

I'm a student of that kind of shit.

111

Take another example. I don't want to shake you up, but right now, right as we're talking, I'm busy studying you. I'm reading up on your body language, how you glance around—you do that a lot incidentally. How you never quite look me in the eyes, how you always focus just to the right or the left. It's like you're afraid to look straight at me. Lots of Caucasians are that way with black people. It's because of the past, because of genocide. It's like they know that we know. You know what I'm saying? So whenever a Caucasian looks a black man in the eye, it's like a guilt trip.

That's the reason I always look straight at them—Caucasians. That's another revolutionary act by the way. You've got your loud revolutions, but also you've also got your quiet revolutions. Day to day shit.

That's also the reason, sooner or later, you're going to have to get real about reparations. The guilt, I mean. That's the reason. And by *you*, I don't mean just you; I mean Caucasians in general. The wealth of America was built on the blood, sweat and tears of the black man. It's like Malcolm used to say: "The black man didn't land on Plymouth Rock. It landed on us!" If it wasn't for slave labor, America would still be like a third world country. And the British would still be running things. Either them, or the French.

Hell, maybe even the Indians!

But yet, on the other hand, reparations is just more bull-shit if you get right down to it. Just more wage capital. I'm talking about robbing a people of their legacy, of the knowledge of who they are. I'm talking about what a black man sees when he looks in the mirror. I'm talking about *pride*. That's what I'm talking about. Sometimes, when I hear Caucasians talk about reparations, I just want to tell them to shove it up their asses. You want to put a price on a black man's pride? I'd trade a million of your damn George Washington dollars, and I'd do it in a second, for the black man to know his rightful place. That's the reason you've got your Five Percent Nation.

Say what?

Africa mentioned the Five Percent Nation? Well, that kind of surprises me because I never think about him as being part of it. I always think about him being among the eighty-five percent—the sheep, in other words. Like when it does finally go down, the Revolution, I mean, he could go whichever way. Eddy's like that too. I figure, eventually, me and Herc will have to set them straight. Get to them before the Dexters of the world do.

That's Africa's brother, Dexter. Total negro. You know what I'm saying? Africa doesn't like to talk much about him.

Why?

Turn off the tape, and I'll tell you why.

It's off?

The reason Africa doesn't talk much about Dexter is because Africa got him killed. Shot dead. Not on purpose, mind you. Accidentally. Dexter was trying to get him out of a situation, and Africa panicked, and Dexter wound up getting shot. I don't know too many details except for that—I don't even think Eddy and Keisha know that much. They just know Dexter got whacked. Herc knows what happened because he was there. In fact, he's the one who told me. He's also the one who got Africa out alive. The only other person who might know what happened is Africa's old man—if Africa told him. Which, by the way, Africa would be a damn crazy fool if he did.

So that's the reason Africa follows Herc around like a puppy dog. At least, that's one of the reasons. Another reason is that people like Africa—they're always looking for something to follow. Something or someone. It's nothing against him. It's just the way he is.

Okay, you can turn your tape recorder back on.

Free Mumia!

But the thing is, I didn't come here to talk about Africa. I came to talk about the Revolution. You know what I'm saying? Now a lot of people, when they think of the Revolution, they only think in terms of black versus white. And it's going to be that, for sure. But the main thing, beyond the black and white thing, is it's going to be a *people's* revolution. The war won't be against the Caucasians *per se.* It will be against the powers that be—who just happen to be mostly Caucasian. It's a class struggle is what I'm saying.

Meanwhile, Caucasians had better sit down and read the Declaration of Independence—there comes a time when revolution becomes a *necessity.* It was a white man who wrote that, Thomas Jefferson!

What?

Well, it's not that complicated, but I'll break it down for you even more. Put it in more personalized terms. When the Revolution comes, if you get in the way, I will kill you. I mean *me,* in particular. And I mean *you,* in particular. The two of us can sit around now, trade ideas like we're doing. Maybe even the two of us can be friends. But if you get in the way, *I will kill you.* And the thing is, it won't even be nothing personal if I do. That's what's so difficult for an intellectual like yourself to comprehend. There's going to come a time, and very soon, when people are going to die . . . not for who they are, not even for what they've done, but for *what they represent.*

I know it's difficult to hear. But there's no turning back at this point. Too much has gone down. Too much blood has been spilled.

That's the reason why reparations is bullshit. It might put off the Revolution for a decade or so—which is why Caucasians will eventually come across with the cash. But in the long run, it's just not going to matter. *Reparations* will not solve *representations.*

We *will* bury you.

Now I know how uncomfortable it is to hear a black man talk like that. It's not *politically,* as they say, *correct.* It would be okay if I was one of those monkey militants, you know, cursing left and right, all antisocial. Then you could just sit back and smile. You could roll your eyes without rolling your eyes; I know how your game is played. But what's uncomfortable, and I can see it in the way you're smiling, is not *what* I'm saying but *how* I'm saying it. You know what I'm saying? I'm getting to you, I'm messing with your Caucasian mind, and it's because there's no *animosity* in my voice.

So I'll say it again.

We *will* bury you.

The only question is: What's going to set it off?

Free Mumia!

Free Mumia!

Free Mumia!

SORRY ABOUT LAST WEEK, BUT I HAD TO GO MEET LIANG'S
MAMA-SAN. Liang don't call her that, but I do. Liang's
Mama-san.

It just fits.

By the way, did Jerome make you do that *Free Mumia!*
shit? I wouldn't pay too much mind to it. It's like a power
trip with him. You know what I'm saying? He makes me
and Fast Eddy do it every time we hang out. Eddy says it's
like a chant, like something he says without even thinking
about it. But I think it's more like a dog pissing to let the
rest of the dogs know where he lives. Really, he don't mean
nothing by it.

The only one he don't pull that shit on is Herc. That's
'cause Herc would bust him up if he tried.

But to get back to Liang's Mama-san, Liang dragged me
out to meet the old cunt last week. That's the reason I sent
Jerome; I knew I couldn't make our regular lunch 'cause I
had to ride out to Flushing. Except the place is so chink,
now I call it *Floo-Shing.*

Yo, I ain't *never* seen a place so chink-ified. Not even
Chinatown. Soon as I stepped out of that Number Seven,
it's like fish-stank off the hook! Made my eyes water. *Word!*
You got fish guts in the gutter. Not fresh fish guts neither.
I'm talking week-old fish guts. Like the chinks just waiting
for it to disintegrate. You got fish guts; plus, you got other
stuff that goes into the stank. Bleach, I think. Plus, rotting
garbage. Vegetables and shit. Plus, I don't know what else.
Nasty!

But the thing is, I think the noise is even worse than the
stank. Cars honking at people. Buses honking at cars. Plus,
chinks jabbering away, yelling at each other in Chinkese. I
think that's what hell must be like. Hell must be run by
chinks 'cause I don't think no one else could make such a
mess of their own place. Say this much for Jews—at least
they neat!

So I start walking towards the address Liang gave me, and I'm passing food markets with like barbecued squirrels and cats hanging in the windows, all skinned and roasted up. Like the sight of their cooked carcasses is what's going to bring the chink customers into the stores.

Plus, the signs in the store windows got chink letters. No English except for maybe a couple of clothes stores. Chink letters and chink decorations, like the toy-looking red tee-pees Godzilla steps on. Even the banks got chink signs. *The banks!* I mean, what do chinks want? Washingtons and Lincolns with slanty eyes? It's just unnatural when things go that much chink!

So I'm walking and walking, and, maybe about fifteen minutes later, I hunt down the address. It's a nice flat house. Looks just like the rest of the houses on the block. People say chink faces look alike, but I think it's chink houses that look alike, even more than chinks faces do, or else maybe it's just that chinks like houses that look alike. It's a kind of chicken and egg thing. Who knows what came first?

So I walk on up to the screen door, and I notice instead of a bell to ring it's got like metal chimes that hang down with a string attached. So I give the string a tug, and the chimes kind of tinkle—it don't seem to me like it's even loud enough to hear inside the house. But I guess Mama-san must be used to it by now 'cause a few seconds later, I hear her footsteps. I know it ain't Liang just from the sound of the footsteps. Quick. You know what I'm saying? Like *chop-chop-chop.* Whereas Liang ain't the type that rushes.

Actually, it's kind of humorous what Mama-san looks like. I mean, well, it wouldn't be humorous except for what Liang looks like. Mama-san looks like your average bent-over chink. But if you compare what she looks like with what Liang looks like, you just got to wonder: *Yo, how did that happen?*

So Mama-san waves for me to come in, and then she's like all bowing and waving, like she's just so happy her daughter's brought home a nigga—which is a joke 'cause it's a well-known fact that chink parents hate niggas worse than what have you. But meanwhile, I ain't never got smiled at so big. That's the one thing alike with Mama-san and Liang. Both of them seem one way on the outside, but inside you know it's a different story.

Inside, you just *know* Mama-san wishes I was hanging from a damn chink tree.

"No English!" she keeps saying, "No English!"

But meanwhile smiling.

Then I hear Liang's voice calling from the backyard. "Africa?"

"Yo!"

"You like barbecue, yes?"

I shout back, "I'm a nigga, ain't I?"

So I walk straight through the flat house and then out back, and I'm grinning stupid already, like I do around Liang; but then, the second I step out on the back porch, it hits me—the red, white and blue. I mean, *yo*, I've seen flags in my day, but this motherfucker is like a *flag*. It's maybe twelve feet long, and it's only about six feet off the ground, and it's flapping around in the wind. So when I say it hit me, I mean it snapped right in front of my face. Missed my left eye by about a inch. Just *snap*. Not to mention what it stands for—I mean, if you're a black man.

That's the flag of the devil. You know what I'm saying?

So right off I got a feeling there's going to be trouble. 'Cause I'm thinking: *Ain't no way I'm chowing down with that thing waving in my face.* It's like as if I was a Jew, and it was a German flag—you know, a swat sticker. Except I just *know* Mama-san's going to shit a brick if I make a big deal out of it.

The thing is, it's like one hundred percent sure Liang only wanted to have a barbecue in the first place to make me sit underneath that damn flag. She could've just as easy cooked inside. I know it's another one of her tests. It's like—oh, I don't even know what it's like. No, wait, it's like I'm looking at the hot dog rolls on the table, and I'm thinking Liang won't be satisfied till she's got my black dick on a hot dog roll.

Meanwhile, Liang's standing over by the grill, poking at the coals. She's got on a light blue tee shirt, no sleeves, and you can see the edges of her titties spilling out the sides; as soon as I see Liang in that tee shirt, the voice inside my head that's saying *No way* changes to *Way.* It shames me to say it, but I'm just flat out whipped. Even before I can start up, I'm whipped. I know I'm going to do it, going to sit down nice and quiet, like a good little nigga, underneath the red, white and blue. If Liang wanted me to sing *Oh Say Can You See,* yo, I'd be right there, doing it, standing straight, right hand over my heart, singing my lungs out!

I walk over to her, and she turns her head so I can kiss her cheek—which is all I got off the bitch in two weeks! It's kind of pathetic, in a way. Kind of sad too. It's sad 'cause me being with Liang is the first thing me and Herc can't even discuss about. Every time I mention her name, he just kind of rolls his eyes. I know he lost respect for me, and I keep telling myself he's right, but that all just kind of gets lost when I get next to her.

But I already gave up on myself when it comes to Liang. That's just the way it is. You know what I'm saying?

It's like, she made me into her bitch.

Now it's about a half hour later. The three of us are chowing down on dogs and burgers, sitting around a wooden picnic table; Liang and Mama-san are sitting on one side, and I'm sitting across from them, scarfing down whatever falls on my plate, grinning like a damn fool—and meanwhile I'm staring up at the red, white and blue. I'm trying not to think about it, but I know, inside my heart, I'm fronting like I ain't never fronted before. What I keep thinking about is what Herc would say if he saw me, and how ashamed he'd be. Jerome, too. Except I don't give a rat's ass whatever Jerome thinks.

Meanwhile, I start noticing Mama-san. She's still got that chink smile going on, and every time she notices me noticing her, she like gives me a little bow with her head.

That's when the first zap comes. It catches me off guard, like *zap!* It's one of those bug things. Zappers, I think they're called. You know . . . the blue light gets 'em curious, bugs I mean, and then, *zap*, they get fried.

Suddenly, Mama-san's smiling even more. Then another bug gets zapped. That just cracks her up! She ain't said a single word in chink or English since we started to eat, but now she's laughing and laughing.

Then comes another zap.

Mama-san reaches across the table and slaps my hand. Like it's a joke, and I ain't getting it! So I look over at Liang, and she's grinning too. Not at the bugs, but at the situation. The fact that her Mama-san's slapping me on the hand, laughing at the bugs, and the fact that I'm fronting. It's like Liang's World. She's got what she wanted, and she just wants to make sure I know it.

Suddenly, she says to me, "Do you see? United States not like how you say. Not like how you think. Like this. The reason come to United States, many people, for this. This United States."

"Except it's the nigga who gets zapped," I say. "That's the United States."

"Why you always say *nigga*? You like word? You think *nigga* more better than *nigger.*"

"I do."

"Why more better?"

"*Nigger* is what a white man calls a black man. *Nigga* is what a black man calls himself."

"Sound same to me," she says. "I think *nigga* and *nigger* same."

"You can think whatever you want. I *know* there's a difference."

She thinks on that a second, then says, "What if I call *nigger?*"

"Don't bother me," I say.

"Why no bother?"

"'Cause I know you don't mean nothing by it."

"But what if pretend I was a white man?"

I give a little laugh. "Then, we going to war."

"It stupid! *Nigga* is *nigger!* Same word!"

"Stop saying it, woman!"

"Why stop? Word hurt you? Only just a word!"

"It *ain't* only a word. That's what I'm trying to say."

"Then why you say word? *Nigga, nigga, nigga* is only what you say."

"Like I said, it's different if I say it."

That's when Mama-san chimes in. "Nigga!"

"What?"

She starts laughing and slaps me on the hand again. "Nigga! Nigga! Nigga!"

I turn back to Liang. "Now you got her doing it!"

Mama-san's about to split her gut, she's cracking up so hard. "Nigga! Nigga! Nigga!"

The thing is, the way she's saying it, it *is* kind of humorous. I mean, it's like *ni-GAH*. You know what I'm saying? It's like *ni-GAH, ni-GAH, ni-GAH*. The way she's saying it, *ni-GAH,* it almost sounds chink. Meanwhile, Mama-san thinks like she's speaking English. Like she's showing off a new trick. *Ni-GAH, ni-GAH, ni-GAH!*

It gets to a point, you just got to laugh.

So finally I kind of shrug at her. "Yo, I give up. You win. *Ni-GAH*. That's what I am. *Ni-GAH.* "

Then, out of the corner of my eye, I catch Liang shooting Mama-san a look. It's so quick I can't even make out what kind of look it was—just that it was a look. Then, just like that, Mama-san stops laughing. Strange. It's like as if Liang hit the *off* switch, and Mama-san all of a sudden clammed up.

That kind of got to me. You know what I'm saying? It got to me, how Liang made Mama-san stop saying *nigga*.

It's like, just when you figure she's getting off cutting you down, she does something nice. It lets you know she's got a heart, even if she don't let on.

Afterwards . . . well, that's the thing. I don't remember too much about what happened afterwards. It was just, I guess, *mellow.* That's the only word for how it was afterwards. It wasn't exactly like we was chillin'. Truthfully, I don't think Liang even knows how to chill. It's like as if she don't got the chillin' chromosome. You know what I mean? That's the thing about chinks. What I mean is, it's *another* thing about chinks.

Chinks don't chill.

But, anyway, afterwards, like I was saying, it got nice and mellow—which is almost as good as chillin'. It's like chillin' except without the rap. It's more like an individualistic thing, being mellow. Whereas chillin' is more like with people. You do a little conversating. That's the main difference. What I'm saying is even though there was three of us in the backyard, me and Liang and Mama-san, it's like we was just three individuals. But yet it was mellow. The sun was shining down. The smell of barbecue was there. It was just mellow.

You know what I'm saying?

It gets to a point, being mellow, where you just naturally close your eyes. Which is what I did. I was laying there on that chair, the kind that folds down flat, and I got my eyes closed, and I got the sun in my face, and then I feel something. At first, I didn't know what it was—I thought it was like a cat or something brushing up against my right hand. But then I felt a squeeze. That's when I knew it was Liang's hand that was squeezing my hand. I didn't open my eyes. I played it cool. You know what I'm saying? I didn't smile. I didn't even squeeze her hand back. I just let the moment be.

Yo, I think that was maybe the sweetest moment of my damn life. Laying in the sun. Liang squeezing my hand.

Being mellow.

Now don't look at me like that. I know it don't make no sense. I know it's just her hand, and it ain't even holding my dick. But that's the whole thing. It's like if a man's in the desert, and he ain't drunk nothing for a week, a Dixie cup of water's going to taste like the best he ever had. It was like that with Liang squeezing my hand. It was like the first time I ever got the sense that she was wanting to be with me.

It *does* sound kind of wack, don't it? If I listen to it myself, it sounds way wack. Even kind of white on top of it. Word up! Like as if I was a wacked out white boy.

But that was what I was thinking at the time. I was thinking like if the world blew up at that second, if it just got too wicked for God to put up with the situation one second longer, I'd be going down happy.

Now the reason I'm saying about what happened in the backyard, what I was thinking and such, is because it just goes to show how easy a brother can get caught up. No matter the kind of person he is. No matter how much knowledge he has. No matter what have you. There's always going to be temptations.

You know what I'm saying?

What I'm saying is you got to distance yourself. You got to take a couple of steps back. Perspective, now *that's* what I'm talking about. 'Cause when you come right down to it, Liang is just a chink ho. Just because of how I feel about her, that don't change nothing. Her cunt don't stink no less than the next cunt. That's what you call the *reality* of the situation. So you can be a romantic, but yet you also got to keep it real.

That's all I'm saying.

NAH, I STILL AIN'T IN THE CUT. That chink bitch got me so twisted up inside, yo, I don't know what's what no more. You know what I'm saying? I don't know if it's even worth it, to be truthful. Being with Liang, I mean. The thing is, I got so much already put in, it don't make no sense to pull out before the deal's done. It's a damn dilemma is what it is.

Before I forget, I may not be able to meet up with you in a couple of weeks. Next week I'm good, but the week after that, I don't know. I just wanted to let you know ahead of time. I won't be for sure until the night before. I know how we said at the beginning about not giving phone numbers, but—

What?

No, nothing like that. Herc's got some business with this Bronx nigga. Just, you know, business. Shit that needs to be put right. That's the date it's got to get done by. The thing is, probably, it ain't even going down. Nothing, I mean. What I mean is, nothing's going down. Niggas'll get on the horn, and the next thing they'll work it out; that's what I'm predicting. But you never know with the Bronx, so he wants me to ride with him.

And I got to do it 'cause, you know, it's *Herc*.

The reason why I'm predicting nothing's going to go down is 'cause Herc wouldn't never ask me to ride if he thought something was going to go down. He kind of looks out for me. On account of what happened with Dexter. Yeah, Jerome told me he told you. The thing is, Jerome's so full of shit, you don't want to take nothing he says too serious. He likes to talk like he knows shit, but he don't know shit. He knows *book* shit, but he don't know *street* shit.

No, it's not like that.

All right, let's just put it like this: A bad thing happened, and Dexter got himself killed. That's all I'm going to say. That's the main thing anyway. That's the entire story.

What?

Heh, heh, not much gets past you, does it? Yeah, you're right again. That *is* the big reason I don't talk to my old man no more. He don't see it like how I see it. Dexter getting himself killed, I mean. My old man kind of holds me to blame. It ain't fair, but, hey, what can you do? He's got his way of looking at things, and I got mine. *Perspective.* That's the word for it. Me and my old man got a different perspective.

Check it out: *Perspective.* It's deep.

If you got perspective, you got power. Take, for an example, how the Bronx shit is giving me perspective on Liang. I've been so busy thinking about what's going down in two weeks, I ain't had time to think about her. Plus, when I do think about her, suddenly, she ain't all that. You know what I'm saying? That's what you call perspective. If you spend too much time thinking about one thing, be it a bitch or a dis or what have you, it gets like *mad* in your brain even if it started out as practically nothing.

I'll give you another example.

When I was like eleven years old, I got caught hopping over a turnstile in the subway. *Hopping a turnstile!* Do you believe that shit? But still this fat ass Irish cop busted me. Called my old man down to the station to take me home. Yo, I knew I was going to get a whipping. *Knew it.* But he don't say nothing, my old man, on the ride home. Then the two of us walk inside, and still nothing. He don't yell. He just kind of breathes heavy. I remember following him to the closet as he hung up his coat, waiting for him to slip off his belt; it's a scary sound, him slipping off his belt, like *thp, thp, thp.* But it don't come, the *thp-thp-thp.* He don't slip off his belt. He just walks past me and sits down on the couch. Then he clicks on the tube. It's like he flat out forgot the reason he'd to come pick me up. Like it just skipped his mind.

Meanwhile, I start to think: *Hey, I caught a break!*

So I head upstairs.

But then, afterwards, like every five minutes or so, I think I hear him on the steps. My heart starts to beat real fast. My hands get sweaty. Except every time it turns out it's just in my brain. He ain't coming up the steps. I look downstairs, and he ain't moved from the couch.

Finally, it's working on me so much that I head back downstairs. I walk real soft, so he don't hear me. He *still* ain't moved from the couch, but now he's kind of talking to himself. Not loud. Just quiet, under his breath kind of words. What catches my eye is what he's doing with his hands. His right hand's balled up into a fist, and he's slapping it into his left hand. Meanwhile, he's talking real low, under his breath, like as if he's talking to his hands when they come together. It's almost like he's praying—except he's praying into his fist.

So I watch him for maybe a minute, and I think maybe he's bugging. You know what I'm saying? Like *bugging*— for real. Like it's the straw that broke the camel.

Finally, I say, "Yo, Dad?"

He don't even look at me. "Not now, Kevin."

"You going to whip me or what?"

"Not now."

"You going to whip me later though?"

"Maybe," he say. "But not now."

Well, I figure "maybe" means he's going to whip me later. So I chill out for a few minutes. Except then I start to think. *Later* could be in an hour, or it could be tomorrow, or it could be next week. Now, suddenly, *I'm* bugging. *Mad* bugging. Like that entire night, and then the next night afterwards, whenever my old man got up to piss in the middle of the night . . . I'd hear him, and I'd start to shake in my bed.

It went on like that for like a week. It got the point where every time I'd hear footsteps in the house, I'd figure I'm going to get my whipping. It was like I was waiting for

126

a d.b.—you know, a drive-by. Except it don't come. And like as if that wasn't bad enough, pretty soon Dex catches on to the situation. So every so often, he'd come stomping up the stairs just to mess with me. Just to get me crazy in the brain.

Finally, you know what happens?

I *asked* for it! The whipping, I mean!

I just couldn't take it no more. So I walked downstairs, and I walked right up to my old man, who was just chilling on the couch, and I said, "I'd like my whipping now."

He kind of smiled at that. "You would, would you?"

"Yeah, I would."

"Why now?"

I think for a second. "To get it over with."

"It's been weighing on your mind, then?"

"Yeah," I said.

"The whipping's been weighing on your mind?"

"Yeah."

"What about the thing that earned you the whipping?"

"Yo, I was just trying to beat the fare."

He kind of shook his head, and then he stood up and started slipping off his belt. As soon as I heard that *thp-thp-thp*, I closed my eyes real tight. The thing is, it wasn't such a bad whipping. I got worse lots of times. It wasn't nothing. But 'cause I thought about it so long, that's what made it so bad. I remember thinking that exact thing while my old man was still whipping me, like: *Hey, this ain't so bad!* Then afterwards I felt dumb stupid. It's like you figure you're going to drown in the ocean . . . except then all that happens is you get pissed on.

So, in a way, I was glad my old man whipped me. 'Cause I got *wisdom* out of it. That's the key. Whatever happens, you got to learn from it.

What?

Yo, I thought I explained about that. I ain't into Liang no more. Or at least not so much. The bitch don't do nothing but criticize. It's fine once in a while; I know I ain't perfect. But, *dag,* it's like she's dogging me every minute the two of us spend together. I don't go for that. You know what I'm saying? I mean, sometimes you want a little show of support. I'll give you a perfect example of exactly what I'm saying. She knows the thing with Herc's got me bugging. So what does she do? Dogs me about it! Talking how Herc ain't a true friend, how he takes advantage. I mean, that's *Herc* she's hating on. I'm down with him a lot longer than I'm down with her, but she just keeps on going, hating on him, right to my face. So finally I say to her that she better back off.

Then she says, "Why back off? Why if truth?"

I shoot back, "What if I was hating on Molly and Sally? You wouldn't take that, would you?"

"If truth, yes."

"You running on and on about truth. What is *truth?* Check it out: I got my way of thinking, and you got yours."

She gives me a sour look, a real chink kind of sour look. "You know what is truth. Truth is truth."

"Well, what I'm saying is that people make up their own truth. They believe whatever they want to believe. You got your truth, and I got mine. I ain't going to judge yours, no matter how fucked up I might think it is, so don't you go and judge mine."

She slaps her fist down on the bench. Oh, I forgot to say, we was sitting in the playground in Central Park. Sitting on one of them green park benches. So, like I said, I told her people make up their own truth, but then she shoots back with, "It is *not* truth, what you believe, if not true."

"Why you getting so bothered about it? What difference if it's true or not? It's what *I* believe. All I'm saying is you should respect what I believe. Especially when it comes to Herc."

"Why is what I ask."

"First of all, you ain't even met the nigga."

"I don't want to meet! Waste my time!"

"Trust me, Herc ain't dying to meet you neither."

"Then no reason to meet," she say.

"I ain't saying you should meet! That ain't what I'm saying!"

It just went on and on like that; I mean, *no* bitch is *that* fine.

You know what I'm saying?

Now the reason we're sitting in the playground—that's like a whole other story. It starts when Liang shows up at my door with her two-year-old nephew. It was like two o'clock in the afternoon when she showed up, and I wasn't even supposed to see her till that night, but she just shows up at my door with the kid. Then she tells me she's got to mind him for a couple of hours. Says it's a family emergency. So I'm like, *Fine, what's that got to do with me?*

Well, she says, she's got a nail appointment at three-thirty.

That's when I start to get the picture.

She wants me to watch the kid while she's off getting her damn fingernails done.

So that's how come we're sitting in the playground on a Saturday afternoon. It's so she can run off to the nail place, which is right near the park, and I can mind the kid for her. It ain't like I minded doing it. He was a cute little dude with his hair all sticking up like a porcupine. His chink name's something like *Wai Shen,* but in English it comes out "Clement." Don't ask me how. I'm just calling him what Liang called him.

Like I said, I didn't mind doing it. But it's the principle of the thing, the way she always takes advantage.

So Liang rolls on out, and then it's just me and Clement in the playground, and he's running around, doing the kind of shit two-year-old nippers do. Running around for no reason. It's like he just gets it in his head to run, and he runs. Sometimes straight. Sometimes in a circle. It's kind of fascinating when you watch it. It makes you wonder what's going on in his brain, why he just suddenly decides to take off. Why he goes left or right when there ain't nothing special he's running after.

I like nippers. I like to watch 'em. That's why I didn't mind looking after him. It's just, like I said, the principle.

Well, a half hour goes by. Now it's getting near the time Liang said she'd be back, and I'm getting bored, and Clement's getting pretty tuckered out—I could tell 'cause every so often he'd kind of look over at me like as if he was wondering if it was time to go. I kind of felt bad for him. He didn't want to stop. It's like part of being a nipper that you got to play till your mamma tells you to quit. Or your dad, or whoever. You just don't stop on your own. Like stopping on your own ain't in your contract. You know what I'm saying?

But the kid's pretty tuckered out. He's mostly just standing in one place, looking around, taking in the sights. But then he gets it in his head to run again, and he takes off . . . and *boom* he runs smack into another nipper, a little white girl. It was kind of comical, actually, how they crashed together—more like a *boink* than a *boom*. The only thing I could compare it to is a couple of hard-boiled eggs bouncing off one another. Both of the nippers wound up on their butts. It stunned 'em for a second, but you could tell neither of 'em got hurt. Then they kind of checked each other out, like as if they was figuring out if it was the kind of thing to cry about or laugh about.

That's when the little white girl decided it's the kind of thing to cry about. She starts wailing, and Clement just sits there and watches her. I'm watching the two of 'em meanwhile, kind of smiling to myself about what happened.

But then, out of nowhere, the little white girl's mother comes running to the rescue, and then the father comes running three steps behind. They were like your dictionary picture of yuppies. They had the tan shorts going on, and the sunglasses, and she had on a tan hat, and he had on a white shirt with a collar. I'm still just kind of watching as the mother grabs up the little girl and hugs her real tight, and the little girl grabs her mamma and right away stops wailing. It was like sensitive, almost. You know, like sentimental, how the little white girl stopped wailing and calmed down to just a sniffle as soon as she was holding onto her mamma.

But then, a couple of seconds afterwards, the father starts yelling at Clement! No shit! Starts yelling, "Did you hit my daughter? Why did you hit my daughter? Is your father here?" I mean, the guy's right up in Clement's face; he's bent over him, woofing right in his face. Naturally, Clement gets scared, and so he starts wailing too. But the guy don't let up. Now he's pointing his finger at Clement and looking around and calling out, "Whose boy is this?"

He don't even notice me standing up; he's looking for a chink.

"Yo!"

Finally, he sees me walking towards him. He looks over his shoulder, like I must be talking to somebody else. Then he turns back around. Except now he ain't in such a yelling mood no more. You know what I'm saying?

"Yo, what's your problem?"

"It's all right," he answers in a real calm voice. "I'm just looking for this boy's father."

Clement runs over to me and hides behind my leg.

"Yo, why you going ape shit on a little nipper?"

"I just wanted to find—"

"How you like it if I go ape shit on you?"

Now the wife puts in her two cents. "We just wanted to find the boy's parents . . . to make sure he wasn't alone."

"Yo, bitch, I didn't ask you."

That gets the attention of the rest of the folks sitting in the playground.

So I cut a quick look at the husband to see if he's got something to say.

He don't.

"That's right, motherfucker. I just called your ho a bitch. You got a problem with that?"

"Look, man, we're not looking for any trouble—"

"*Look, man?* What year is this? Fucking 1969?"

"Now, look—"

"Back the fuck up before I fuck up your yuppie ass!"

He just stares at me for a couple of seconds, like he don't want to look like a chump in front of so many people, but then the wife kind of takes his hand and pulls him away. Meanwhile, I'm staring him down and staring him down— like as if to say, *"What?"*

Afterwards, Clement's still holding onto my leg. He's peeking around me every so often just to make sure the yuppies are gone, and I know if I walk back to the bench I'm going to wind up dragging him with me. So I just stand there, in the middle of the playground, with my arms folded, with Clement tugging on my left leg. Now let me ask you a question: Ain't that a damn fool predicament for a black man to wind up in? Standing in the middle of a playground, being tugged on by a chink nipper!

That's what happens when you let bitches get the upper hand, when you start thinking with your dick and not with your mind.

But to go back to the story, you know what the joke of it was? That white man, he was like about twice as big as me. He probably could've whupped my ass if he had a mind to do it. But white people don't think like that. It goes back to what I was saying about how white people don't never honk their horns at no nigga. That's 'cause when white people look at a nigga, they don't see what he *is.* They see what he *might do.* You know what I'm saying? Even if white people tell themselves, in their brains, a black man's just like them, he's just a human being, even if they tell themselves he's got blood in him like they do, even if they tell themselves they down with him 'cause they listen to rap and wear Michael Jordan sneakers, they still being racists 'cause it ain't natural. They got to *tell* themselves. What I'm saying is it don't come from the heart. In their heart, white people never stop thinking: *What's the crazy nigga going to do?*

What I'm saying is the yuppies in the playground—they didn't see no human being getting up in their faces. What they saw was a nigga getting crazy. That's the scariest thing in the world for white people. They just can't deal with it. Look at it another way. Suppose I was white or chink. You think that big old white boy would've backed off like he did? But I'm a crazy badass nigga, so who knows what I might do?

It's like what happened with me and Herc and the two faggots. The ones we *didn't* rob, I mean. Not the ones we fought. It didn't matter that we told them we weren't robbing them. They didn't hear the words 'cause they'd already worked it out in their brains what we were going to *do*—which was rob them. So they handed over their bills.

You know what's the funniest thing? It's like when I'm doing business . . . *you know.* And some white boy comes up to me on the corner, and he's like, *Yo, dawg, what up!*

I just get this grin on my face; I can't help it.

Then I say, "Yo, my *main* man!"

That's when the white boy just lights up; he figures he savvies the lingo, so we down. Then I know for sure we going to do business. It don't matter what kind of quality I'm holding. We going to do business 'cause he wants to think he down with me.

That's what white boys live for. Feeling like they down with niggas.

It's a strange kind of thing if you stop and think about it. You might say it's kind of *paradoxical*—how white boys always like to think they down with niggas. It's humorous. 'Cause they ain't, really. They think they are, but they ain't. The funniest thing is hoops. You head down to the West 4th

Street courts, watch for a couple of hours. Sooner or later, you bound to see a white boy call next. It ain't like brothers going to say no. You know what I'm saying? White boy calls next, he got next. That's just how it works.

So a white boy calls next, he got next.

Except then, soon as he starts warming up, suddenly, he's Vanilla Ice. He's got the roll going on—you know, how brothers walk. He got the roll, and he got the head bobbing up and down. He's *yo*-ing left and right.

It's just plain humorous.

REMEMBER THE FIRST QUESTION YOU EVER ASKED ME—YOU KNOW, *DID TAWANA TELL THE TRUTH?* I figure by now I owe you a straight answer. I mean, given what we're doing. Given how we're getting the truth out. So: Did Tawana tell the truth? The answer's no. That's on the real.

You know what I'm saying?

She didn't tell the truth 'cause she was afraid her mamma would whup her ass. The reason why her mamma was going to whup her ass is 'cause she was turning tricks. It ain't no secret.

Why not say so?

Well, you know, it's like a black thing—not saying what you know is real 'cause it's your people. It's like what happens with wolves. When one of the wolves gets injured, you know, gets scratched up by a mountain lion or some such thing, the rest of the wolves form a circle. They let the hurt wolf get healed up. It's like that if you're a black man in America. I mean, the mountain lions been scratching up your people for so long, you just start to feel like you should circle up. It's like a reflex. That's when it's hard to keep it real. You *want* to keep it real. But you got another voice inside of you saying circle up.

What?

That's right, you got me. It's like that with O.J. too. Furman set him up, no doubt, but I don't see how he could've *not* whacked that bitch. I mean, he got cuts on his hands. He got blood in his car. He got a history with her— that's the main thing. But still, irregardless, Furman set him up. It's like the cocksucker couldn't do the right thing, couldn't play it straight.

When you get right down to it, that's all black folks ever wanted. You know what I'm saying? The so-called *level playing field.* You give the black man a level playing field, and he's going to outdo the white man nine times out of ten.

It's the way of the world, the nitty to the gritty. I'm talking *chromosomes*. You got black chromosomes and white chromosomes fighting it out, so who's going to win? The black chomosome! That's how come if you put together one black parent and one white parent, the baby's going to be black.

Now *that's* on the real.

But the thing is, that's the reason there ain't never going to be no level playing field. 'Cause it would be the end of the white race. Chinks too, for that matter. Even spics, it ain't no different. No people on earth can stand up to the black race. It's in the chromosomes.

That's the damn tragedy of the thing right there—how ain't nobody can stand up to the black man, but yet you got niggas whacking one another 'cause of a damn dis. Not even a dis. Just a *maybe* kind of dis. It's just ill. You know what I'm saying? It's like: *I heard that you heard that I heard.* . . . That kind of shit. It don't make no sense.

You know what's funny?

The way I'm talking, that's just how Dexter used to sound. He'd go off on a topic, and then there was no shutting him up. It's funny how, as you get older, you start to hear stuff in a different way. Yo, I mean, Dex had his faults. He was mad in love with the white man, thought the white man was all that and a bag of chips 'cause he freed the slaves. He studied up on the Civil War. Not in school even—I'm talking on his own, he studied up. You should've heard him. He could name you the generals on both sides, North and South, plus their wives' names, plus how many kids they had. Plus, he could name you like every battle, right down to the day of the week it happened. It was freaky. But that was his thing. The nigga even carried around a picture of Lincoln! *Word!* He kept it in his wallet. Plus, also, on the back of the picture was the entire Williamsburg Address. I ain't never seen writing so teensy-weensy! You could hardly even read it. But that didn't matter to Dex 'cause he had the thing memorized inside his brain.

So one time, after he whipped out the picture, I came right up and asked him how come he don't carry around a picture of the Honorable Elijah Muhammad, and you know what he said to me? "Same reason I don't carry around a picture of Mr. Magoo."

Now that's plain disrespectful! Even Liang wouldn't talk to me like that.

Even saying that, though, she got real close just a couple of nights ago.

It's the thing with Herc—you know, that Bronx thing. I mean, she *knows* I'm bugging about it, so she's bugging about it, and it don't do no good either of us bugging 'cause it's Herc, and I got his back irregardless. Ain't no female going to change that. I got Herc's back, and he got mine.

So Liang and me shooting back and forth for hours, just wandering around, the Village, Chinatown, down there. We got nowhere to go is what I'm saying, but we shooting back and forth, and she's talking and talking about Herc, and she's cutting him down like usual, hating on him every which way, and I'm sticking up for him 'cause he's my dawg, and then finally she says, "You love him so much, I think maybe you are homosexual."

That made me laugh, which got her even madder.

"Yes, I say you are homosexual! You and your friend do sex together! Homosexual is what both of you are!"

"Yo," I shoot back, still kind of smiling, "if I was a damn homosexual, why would I bother with you?"

She didn't answer me. Just kind of huffed.

So I said, "Look, it's a black thing. It's like what goes on in a family. You know what I'm saying? I ain't asking you to like it. I ain't even asking you to understand it. I'm only asking you to live with it. It's just the way it is. Reality—that's what I'm talking about."

Then, suddenly, she looks at me different, real serious, real squinty-eyed. Even for a chink, I mean. It was the kind of look that told me I better listen 'cause she's about to lay down the law.

"If you go," she says, "we break up."

"Break up?"

"If you go."

"What you talking 'break up'? Break up *what?* We ain't even done nothing yet!"

"Then you go!"

"You *telling* me not to go?"

"I telling you *go!*"

"Yo, I don't take orders from no one! Not from you. Not from no bitch."

"Then I say go!"

"Plus, especially, I don't take orders from no don't-put-out bitch!"

"Then go!"

"I *will* go. That ain't even in doubt."

"And we break up."

"You ain't listening to me!" I shoot back. "What I'm asking is: *How can we break up when we ain't been together?* It don't make no sense."

That's when it happens. No warning, no nothing. It just happens. Me and Liang standing on the corner of Canal and Broadway, shooting back and forth, and then like a second later she's got her arms wrapped around me, and she's Frenching me—I ain't hardly even kissed her before, but now suddenly she's Frenching me, got her tongue working, doing its thing, and the two of us just standing on the corner of Canal and Broadway, going at it.

Fuck, no—I ain't leaving out nothing! That's exactly how it happened!

It's like one second we shooting, the next we Frenching on the corner!

I mean, the bitch caught me so off guard I couldn't even get into it. You know how sometimes you feel like you're floating over the thing that's going on—like you're you, but yet at the same time you're also you looking down on you? That's what it felt like. Like there was two of me. There was the Africa getting Frenched, and the Africa watching Africa get Frenched.

Except then, all of a sudden, she stops.

She steps back, and she looks me straight in the eye. "*Now,* we break up!"

I just shake my head. "*Damn,* woman!"

"Now we kiss. Now can break up. Now makes sense, yes?"

The way I felt right then . . . it pains me bad to admit it, but I almost felt like maybe I could blow off the Bronx thing. I mean, *the way she looked*—she was wearing one of them tight shirts that ties up in the back, the kind where you can't wear a bra with it, and her titties were hard 'cause of how we just Frenched, and I could see her nips through the shirt. But it wasn't just the titties. It was the whole package. It was Liang. Like you could put her titties on another bitch, and they'd just be fly titties, and that would be the end of the story. You know what I'm saying? Titties is titties. But the whole package, it was like hurting my heart to give it up.

She knew what I was thinking too, what I was feeling in my heart. *Knew.* I say that 'cause she looked me straight in the eye again—that was her way when we were conversating—and said, "Maybe you *don't* go with your friend?"

"Don't do me like this, Liang."

"You don't go? Or do? Which?"

"He's my *dawg,* Liang. I got to go."

"I once have dog. He just dog."

"What I mean is: he's my *brother.*"

"So which one? Brother or dog?"

"He's my *blood,* Liang. I can't say it no clearer."

"Anyway, anyway, anyway! You choose now!"

I stared at her real hard, for a long time. I still thought maybe she might take pity on a brother if she saw how bad I felt. But then, after a few seconds of nothing, I knew it wasn't going to happen.

I turned and left her standing on the corner.

Yo, it still hurts just to talk about it. It feels like a hole. I don't know how to explain it, exactly. It feels like I missed out on what was supposed to be, like my future's going to happen without me.

I was feeling so low after that, I got it into my mind to call Tanya. It's a sure sign when I'm down that I start thinking about Tanya and DeWayne—that's my son, you know, in 201. Jersey, I mean. I don't remember if I told you his name. I don't *like* the name.

What?

That's right; I did tell you about DeWayne.

So the thing with Liang had got me down, and plus the Bronx thing, so I got a desire to call Tanya. It's like that was the first train I missed, and Liang was the second. I phoned up Tanya that night, and I asked her could I swing by and play with DeWayne. I didn't want to take him out or nothing. Just play with him—you know, pick him up and such.

I know it didn't make no sense. But it's how I said last week: I like nippers. It's like me and nippers go together. It's happened where strange nippers come up to me on the sidewalk and grab onto my hand. For no reason. They just kind of take a shine to me.

But Tanya, she don't want no part of me. Her voice gets all hushy, like she don't want to wake up the baby, but yet she's real mad I called. "Who do you think you are?"

"I ain't looking for nothing. I just want to see my boy."

"*Your* boy? DeWayne isn't *your* boy."

Then I'm like, "You know what I mean, Tanya."

"You had your chance, Kevin. It's already come and gone. He's two years old!"

"I don't want another chance. I just want to see *DeWayne.*"

"You can't even say his name without sounding sarcastic!"

"I don't mean to, Tanya. I don't mean nothing bad. I swear I just—"

"No, Kevin!"

Well, it went back and forth like that for maybe a half hour. But the thing is, Tanya's always had a soft spot for me. She don't let on; it's a situation of female pride. You know what I'm saying? But in the end, she came around. Said I could swing by the next day. She told me to come around dinner time—but don't expect no meal or nothing.

Yo, I was *psyched*. Couldn't think of nothing else for the rest of that night. Couldn't move nothing . . . you know, *merchandise*. Couldn't kick it with the niggas on Eighth. Couldn't chill. The next morning, I bought a stuffed bear for DeWayne; it was the biggest motherfucker in the whole store. Then I waited till the afternoon and hopped the PATH Train for Jersey. I knew I was going to be white-boy early, but it got to a point where there wasn't no use hanging around, doing nothing, watching the clock move.

So I'm riding the train, and the bear's taking up a whole entire seat by itself; like I said, it was a big old bear. White folks be grinning at me 'cause of it. They figure a nigga with a stuffed bear must be, you know, safe. Like, *domesticated*. But the thing of it was, I didn't mind whatever they were thinking. Most of the time, it would've pissed me off—I probably would've done shit just to fuck with 'em. But riding out to Jersey, to be honest, it felt kind of good, how they was grinning at me 'cause they figured I was bringing home a teddy bear for my kid. I know it sounds peculiar. I'm just telling you how I felt.

Meanwhile, it's like two hours before the time I'm supposed to be there, and I'm standing on the stoop of Tanya's apartment. She lives upstairs of a hardware store; her father used to own it, but then he sold out and moved away. To Carolina, I think. Or maybe Georgia. I don't know who he sold out to, but Tanya's still got the apartment upstairs.

Besides, it don't matter.

So I'm standing on the stoop, and I'm wondering should I ring the bell or maybe should I go wait for another hour.

But I can't go nowhere or do nothing 'cause I got that big old bear with me—which is why I decided to just go ahead and ring the damn bell.

It takes Tanya about a minute and a half to come to the door, and when she does, she ain't too pleased to see me. "Damn, Kevin! Don't you know how to tell time?"

"It ain't a *thang,* baby cakes. I just figured I'd swing by a little early."

"But it's not time. I'm still not ready. DeWayne's not ready."

"What do you mean, 'DeWayne's not ready'? What's he got to get ready for? I'm his daddy. He was born 'cause of me."

"Dammit, Kevin!" she said, except real soft. "Do I have to spell it out for you?"

That's when it hit me. "You got a nigga up there?"

"I have a *man* upstairs, yes."

"You bring a nigga into my son's house?"

"It's *my* house, Kevin. Your son lives here."

"Yo, that's fucked up. You *know* that's fucked up, Tee."

She sets her hands on her hips and stares me down. "I know it's none of your business."

I take a deep breath. It ain't an argument I'm going to win. You know what I'm saying? "Look, it don't matter. Just bounce the nigga out, and I'll wait down the block."

"It's not that easy, Kevin."

"Sure it's that easy! Just tell the fool to hit the road!"

"Kevin, he *lives* here."

That kind of sucked the breath out of me. I just shook my head.

She took hold of my hand, like as if to make sure I was all right. "I told him you were coming by, and he's got no problem with it—"

"*He's* got no problem with it!"

"He'll be out of the house in a half hour. That's what the two of us had planned. None of this would have happened if you'd showed up when you were supposed to."

"Just answer me this, Tanya. Does DeWayne call him *Daddy*?"

"Does it matter?"

"No bullshit," I say. "Does DeWayne call that nigga *Daddy*?"

She shakes her head. "No, Kevin, he doesn't."

"You lying to me, Tanya?"

"No."

"'Cause I ain't going to take DeWayne calling nobody *Daddy* except for me."

"DeWayne calls him 'Lala' . . . that's how he says *LeShon*."

"LeShon? *LeShon?* What kind of fool name is that?"

"It's his name. That's all," she says. "Now go away and come back in a half hour. On second thought, make that forty-five minutes. I'm not going to rush the man out of his own home on your account."

Then she turns around and heads back upstairs. It's just me and the bear on the stoop again.

What I'm thinking inside my head is: DeWayne ain't going to call no dumb ass nigga *Daddy*. He only got one daddy, and that's me. I know it don't make no sense—me thinking that, I mean. I ain't been no daddy to him, ain't even seen him since the day he got born, so it ain't no big thing when you stop and think about it. You know what I'm saying? It's just a word. It don't change nothing. But right about then, it seemed like a big thing.

Yo, I saw DeWayne get born!

Now I had half a mind, at that point, to duck in the bushes—you know, just to check out the motherfucker. LeShon, I mean. The nigga *can't* be all that. If he was, then what's he want with a bitch like Tanya? What I mean is I wouldn't never raise no kid that wasn't mine. I don't care how fine the mama is. What's the point? It's like with used cars. The bottom line is, you just buying some other nigga's headache.

But, then again, I got the bear, so I can't do the bushes. Plus, when you come right down to it, I got no real beef with LeShon. Truthfully, I'm glad Tanya's with somebody. It's for sure I didn't love her—or else I would've told her so when DeWayne got born. You always got to have perspective. So, yeah, I wish Tanya nothing but the best. If this LeShon motherfucker makes her happy, hey, I'm happy for her.

It's all good.

So I toted the bear back to the train station, and I sat and waited for almost an hour, just thinking, just remembering, and then I headed back for Tanya's place. She's watching out the window as I walk up the stoop; I don't even got to ring the bell again. She pokes her head out the door, and now it's like nothing happened, like I never showed up early, 'cause she's got a smile about a mile long. Then she opens the door the rest of the way.

That's when I saw my boy.

Yo, I couldn't hardly believe it! He was such a little fry when I saw him in the hospital; I could've palmed him like it was nothing. Now, he was standing next to his mama, hiding behind her legs, peeking out from around her butt. He was like a full grown nipper. He had the plastic sucker going in his mouth, the curly hair, the pajamas with the feetsies in 'em. He could've been on television; that's how cute he looked.

Finally, Tanya pushes him out from behind her. "DeWayne, I want you to say hello to Kevin. Can you do that for Mommie?"

DeWayne looks up at me; he's still scared. He opens up his mouth, and the sucker drops right out. He stares at it on the floor for a second, then looks up at me again. Now he's like moving his lips, but nothing's coming out. No sound. Then, just when I figure he ain't going to do it, he raises up his right hand and squeezes it open and closed. It's his way of saying hello.

It about breaks my heart, he's so cute doing it.

Then Tanya pats him on the head. "He's a late talker. The doctor says it's nothing to worry about."

"Maybe he just don't got nothing to say."

Tanya gives a little laugh. "Maybe that's it."

I squat down so I can look him in the eye. "That the reason you don't talk, nigga? 'Cause you don't got nothing to say?"

DeWayne steps back a second, then steps forward again 'cause he's curious. He reaches out with his little right hand and checks me out. He feels my nose and mouth, then my 'do. His skin's so soft, it feels like pussy.

Meanwhile, I pick up his sucker and hand it back to him.

He gives me a big smile. He's about to stick it back in his mouth, but his mama snatches it away. Then she starts laughing. "No, baby, it's dirty. Mommie will get you a clean one."

The thing is, he don't even mind her taking away his sucker. He's too busy concentrating on me, checking me out, smiling real big.

Then Tanya says, "You can pick him up if you want. He likes being picked up."

Well, I think on it; actually, it's like the entire reason I rode out to Jersey. But then, all of a sudden, I'm like, "Nah."

"He won't break, Kevin."

"It ain't that. I'm just not in the mood."

Except now it's too late. DeWayne's already heard her say *pick up,* and he knows what that means, so now he's got his heart set on it. He's like pawing at me, jumping up on his tiptoes, waiting for the ride.

Truthfully, I don't even know where to grab him. I kind of reach for his waist, but then he lunges forward till I catch hold of him under his shoulders. That's how smart my boy is—he figured out that I didn't know what I was doing, so he *made* me pick him up the right way.

So now I got him in my arms, and he's gurgling and laughing, and making noises like babies do, and meanwhile

I almost forgot about the bear that's sitting out on the stoop. DeWayne ain't even peeped it yet 'cause I kind of set it down behind me when Tanya cracked open the door.

"Yo," I whisper to him, "I got a present for you, nigga. You want to see what I got for you?"

He gets it too. He knows what I'm saying. He starts clapping his hands together like he can't hardly wait.

Soon as he catches sight of that bear, he wants to go down and check it out. So I set him down, and he stares for a couple of seconds. It's way bigger than he is. He don't know quite what to make of it. But then, out of nowhere, he hauls off and bops it right in the nose. Just wails on it, *boom!* Then he turns back around to me and his mama to see if we mad, but we ain't, so then he turns back around and gives the bear another shot, right in the nose. Then he starts laughing and laughing.

Then I start laughing. "You going to be a real badass you get bigger, ain't you?"

"No, he's going to be a lawyer," his mama says.

That makes me laugh some more. "Then he's going to have to sue the shit out of his own self, 'cause it's for sure he's going to be a badass motherfucker. *No doubt.*"

DeWayne likes the sound of what I said. He starts clapping again.

But Tanya, she just frowns. "You're never going to grow up, are you Kevin?"

The way she says it, so superior, reminds me of how she was when we was together. It kinds of pisses me off, but I just swallow what I want to say. I mean, I got what I wanted. I got to see my boy. Why ruin it?

To make a long story short, I stuck around for maybe an hour. I didn't talk to Tanya too much, but me and DeWayne, by the end, we regular homies. We played that slapping game, where he puts his hands flat on mine, and then I quick slap down on the backs of his hands before he can pull 'em clear. Except of course I don't slap him hard 'cause he's just a nipper. He *loves* that game! After a while, he don't even wait for me to put my hands down. He just runs up and slaps me. He ain't even particular to slap my hands neither. He's just slapping away at my legs, my arms, wherever he can reach.

Yo, I don't care a rat's ass what Tanya says. That boy's going to be a badass motherfucker!

Towards the end, I start thinking about how I'm missing out on my boy's growing up, and it kind of makes me sad. Which is natural, I guess. But the truth is, it makes me sad, but not too sad. I ain't into that diaper shit, and I know that's part of what it means being a daddy. So, in a way, an hour was enough. I got a taste of what it's like. I got a big old hug from DeWayne when I stood up to go. That's what I went to Jersey for in the first place. . . .

Hey, you want to see something?

Check it out.

Well, it ain't a twelve gauge. That's for sure. But the motherfucker'll do the job.

Actually, it's a Glock. Nine millimeter, semi-automatic, .33 clip. German engineering at its finest. I got it from Herc—which is the reason how I know he's serious about tomorrow night 'cause he knows I don't like packing. But it's like the old saying:

Gotta get a gat
To get a lotta got.

Truthfully, though, I ain't even held a piece in my hand since the night Dex died. Yeah, I know. You been dying to find out the details since the beginning, so now I'm going to tell you.

Why?

I don't know why. I guess I just feel agreeable right now. I mean, yo, the two of us been working on this damn project for like three months. It ain't like we *friends* or nothing; I ain't kidding myself. All I'm saying is I know you're curious about what happened to Dexter. I know it's been preying on your mind, so now I decided to tell you. That's all I'm saying.

Well, the first thing you got to know is that Dex is six years older than me. *Was* six years older—now, he ain't nothing. The second thing is that my mama died when I was twelve; she caught leukemia, and then she died. What happened, basically, is that Dex took it on his self to raise me up—like he was my mama. I don't mean nothing faggy. He just figured my old man was busy with work, so he started watching out for me. But also, at the same time, he started bossing me around. Telling me where I could and couldn't hang. Telling me who I could and couldn't hang with. I can look back now and realize he did it out of love, but back then it seemed like he was being bossy 'cause he liked it. You know what I'm saying? 'Cause he was bigger than me, he figured he could boss me around. That's what it seemed like to me.

It got to a point, over the years, where if Dex didn't like what I was doing, he'd just come down to wherever I was at and haul my ass back home. Now it's one thing him doing that when I was just a young whippersnapper and he's way bigger than me. Like when I was twelve and he was eighteen. Then it's like older brother shit. But it's a whole other story when I'm grown up myself and got a life of my own; I'm talking when I'm sixteen years old, and he's still tracking me down and busting me in front of my dawgs. I mean, how you going to get respect on the street if your older brother disrespects you like that?

Well, basically, what happened is Dex came after me one night in Bed Stuy—I mean, the nigga was so naive he didn't even know that's the Killing Fields. He figured he'd just roll on in, like usual, and haul my ass home. He meant well, but he got himself involved in shit he should've let be. To make a long story short, he got himself whacked.

Huh?

What's the point? You already know how the story ends. He got himself whacked.

Fine, you want to know, I'll tell you.

It was past midnight, and me and Herc was looking for a nigga that Herc was supposed to set me up with. It was a connection. *Business.* That kind of connection.

So we asking around. Niggas out on their stoops, friendly enough, pointing out where they think Herc's nigga is at, but we walking and walking and can't find him nowhere. After maybe an hour, we start getting a feeling like something ain't right; it's like the nigga's purposely staying one step ahead of us, hanging around just long enough to keep the trail warm, then taking off, running us around Bed Stuy. Probably, we should've just took off ourselves. That's what I wanted to do, but Herc kept saying how this nigga's The Don—like once you was in with him, you was in period.

So we walking and walking, and it's coming up on 1:30 in the a.m., and that's when it starts to go down. Hardly nobody's outside on the stoops no more, and the last directions we got pointed us to an abandoned building. Yo, I didn't like the look of the place the second I laid eyes on it. I mean, it looked like one of those bombed-out buildings like you see in World War Two flicks. Walls half knocked down, with lots of loose bricks out on the sidewalk. Broken glass all over—I'm talking foot-long sheets of it. There was even a smashed-up stove out on the front lawn. But when we get up close, we can hear voices inside. Plus, there's like a fire and a flicker of blunts. So Herc looks at me, and I look at him, and it's like the two of us just kind of shrug.

"Yo!" Herc calls out.

Then comes the answer. "Yo, yourself!"

So Herc calls out his nigga's name.

"Hercules?"

"Yo!"

"Who you brung with you?"

"Kevin."

"That the one you told me about?"

"Yeah."

"Walk through the doorway on your right, the red one. Lots of glass, so watch your step."

So we go inside the place—and to tell you the honest truth, I was probably more scared the motherfucker was going to come right down on our heads than whatever business we was going to do. I mean, it wasn't just the glass. It's the floor; it's creaking every step we take, plus the air is filled with dust like as if a wall just collapsed five minutes ago.

Finally, we come to the main room. I mean, it was probably part of the ground floor lobby, but now its blocked off from the sidewalk by piles of bricks and shit. Seven or eight niggas is there, and they got a wood fire going inside a trash can. It's spooky, the way the fire makes the niggas look. Shadows. You know what I'm saying? Like you can't quite see no one's face, but yet you get flashes of their eyes.

So Herc says *Yo!* again, only softer, and then he walks up to the head nigga. He's real obese, the head nigga, almost like one of those Richard Simmons dudes, like Jabba the Hut. What gets me is how the floor don't cave in where he's at. Naturally, he don't stand up; he ain't thc standing up type, but now he ain't going to stand up irregardless 'cause he's like the godfather. You know what I'm saying? Like Herc's got to kiss his ring. I don't mean *actually* kiss his ring. But Herc's got to come to where he's at. He ain't going to stand up and come to Herc. It's a respect thing, like a ceremony. Like as if to say: *Now you in Bed Stuy World, which is my world, so you got to come with mad props.*

Meanwhile, I don't know if I'm supposed to follow Herc or wait, so I just wait. The two of them whisper back and forth for a few seconds; then the head nigga glances over at me. He starts grinning, a real fat grin.

"What you scared of, little brother? I ain't going to bite you."

The rest of the niggas laugh hard at that. I laugh too. It *is* kind of humorous, how I was just standing there, doing nothing.

I walk up to him and say, "Yo."

"I hear you got *beaucoup* plans."

I nod at him, like: *That's right.*

"*Beaucoup* plans need *beaucoup* dollars. You know what I'm saying?"

"I know," I say.

"If I can set you up for *beaucoup* dollars—and I ain't saying I'm going to but *if I can*—you down with that?"

"You *know* I'm down with that."

That cracks him up. "Skinny little bro's got *cahones*, don't he?"

That cracks up the rest of the niggas. I start laughing too even though it ain't very funny to me, kind of a dis.

But then the head nigga suddenly stops laughing, and then all of a sudden so do the rest of 'em. It's like as if somebody grabbed the remote and hit the *mute* button.

"The question is," the head nigga says, "can I trust you?"

I nod again, trying to look real serious.

"Hercules *says* I can trust you, but I've had bad experience with high school shorties. Why do you think I should I trust you?"

I look him square. "'Cause I'm trustable."

"Says you!"

"Ain't no one else saying different."

He starts to smiling again. Yo, I can tell he likes me.

Except that's when it happens. The evil shit, I mean.

I hear a voice out on the street. "You in there, Kevin?"

It takes me a second to realize it's Dex. He's standing in front of the house, on the sidewalk, calling after me like as if I was still twelve years old, like as if I was rolling with the homies down the block. Man, it's *Bed Stuy!* But he come

151

after me irregardless, like as if I was rolling with the homies.

"Kevin, you better get your ass out here the time I count to ten. You heard me?"

"Oh shit!" Herc says. "Oh shit!"

I turn to the head nigga. He's staring me down. "Did you bitches fuck us?"

"No way, man. That's just my brother—"

"You fucked us, didn't you? You bitches fucked us!"

"Don't nobody move!" Herc yells.

So I spin back around.

Herc's got his .38 whipped out, and he's waving it at everybody at once. He's got this crazy look in his eye. That's about when I realize what's going down. The two of us is fucked—I mean, we ain't fucked *yet,* but it's for sure we ain't walking out the way we came in. My heart starts beating real fast, and for a second I can't move my feet.

Then Herc screams, "Yo, *Kev!*"

That snaps me out of it, and I jump behind Herc.

"Don't nobody move," he says again, this time calmer.

The rest of the niggas hold their ground.

"Here." Herc whips out another piece and slaps it in my left hand; that scared the shit out of me even more, how he slapped it, like a runner passing a stick in a race. But I got hold of it, and I started waving it like he was doing. I didn't point it at nobody, just kind of waved it. It sounds funny to say, but I didn't want nobody to take it personal.

The thing is, the niggas didn't seem too pissed off. I mean, considering. The head nigga was kind of sighing, like as if to say he should've known better. Then me and Herc started to back out.

We took slow steps at first, backwards steps, but then we turned the first corner, and that's when we took off. Except, like I said, there was bricks and shit lying all around on the floor. It was about the second or third step I took after I turned; I tripped over something; I think maybe it was a cinder block. But I tripped over it and fell, and when I hit the floor it knocked the gun out of my hand, and it went off. That's what started it.

"Motherfucking bitches!" the head nigga screams.

See, he thought we was shooting at him. But it was just the .22 I dropped going off. That's how it started. Me dropping the .22. Right off, about ten rounds come back at us. They ricocheting all around, and Herc's grabbing my arm, trying to yank me up, and meanwhile he's shooting back at the same time. But the thing is, I fell on glass, so now I'm cut up on my left side; I can feel myself bleeding, and it don't sink in that I fell on glass—I figure somehow I got shot! That scares me even more, so I don't want to move.

So now Herc's dragging me along the floor, and he's shooting into walls, and his bullets is ricocheting, and the niggas is shooting back, and their bullets is ricocheting, and it's just total confusion.

"Get up! Get up!" Herc's yelling.

But I'm like, "I"m hit! I'm hit!"

"You ain't hit!"

"I'm hit! I'm hit!"

"Damn it, Kev! You ain't hit!"

He lets go of me, and he starts running. The weird part is, the second Herc lets go of me, I realize he's right: I *ain't* hit. So maybe a second later I jump up and start running after him, and then, after maybe another ten seconds, I catch up to him, and then the two of us tearing ass out across the front lawn, and meanwhile the bullets still ricocheting behind us, so we don't stop. Just keep running. Maybe six or seven blocks.

That's when I remember about Dex.

I stop in my tracks. "We got to go back."

Herc turns and just stares at me. "What?"

"We got to go back! We left Dexter!"

"You crazy, nigga? We can't go back!"

"We *got* to!"

"Dexter caused the whole thing. We *ain't* going back for him."

"He's my *brother,* Herc."

"What he ever do for you? Except get you shot at just now? He show you respect? Name one time he ever showed you respect, and then we'll go back for him. Once is all I'm asking. One time he ever showed you respect."

I couldn't do it.

Herc says in a soft voice, "He be okay, Kev. He just a nigga to them, no one special."

The thing is, even if we did go back, what we going to do? Herc had like three rounds left in his clip, and I never picked up the .22 after I dropped it. So what we going to do? Grab a few bricks and charge the front door? Wasn't nothing we could've did even if we *did* go back.

Plus, it's like I said. Dex had no business doing what he did. You know what I'm saying? Tracking me down like I was a runaway slave. That's how little respect he showed me. Like as if I was his slave. Why he didn't show me no more respect than that? I was his *brother.* You know what I'm saying? I was his flesh and blood, and he don't show me no more respect than a runaway slave. But yet, even so, if I didn't drop the damn .22, I *still* would've gone back. Even with how he treated me.

Yo, I wouldn't *never* have left him to die on that front lawn.

You know what I'm saying?

Yo, I'm asking: *Do you know what I'm saying?*

It was just fucked up, the entire thing. I mean, it was almost comical how fucked up it was. What happened was Dex went running into the building after he heard the first shots. Anyway, that's what the police said, so you can take it with like a grain of sand. It don't matter anyway 'cause, whatever happened, me and Herc never saw him when we was running out. There was so many ways in, around broke-down walls and such, and he must've took a different one.

We never saw him. The last thing I ever heard him say was how I better get my ass out. That's the last fucking memory I have of him. "You better get your ass out here the time I count to ten." Those were the last words he said to me.

He got gutshot and died.

The police eventually picked up a couple of the niggas—not 'cause of me though. They showed me lots of photos, and I just shook my head. Actually, the one photo I did recognize was the head nigga—who it turns out his real name is Lamar. But I didn't say nothing. I ain't going to roll over on no brother, especially since he only did what he felt like he had to do. I mean, a nigga's got a right to do what he's got to do. Even so, a couple of the niggas did eventually get picked up. There was a trial; I said my piece. I didn't give up nobody. Plus, no one knew, not even the niggas themselves, who fired the shot that killed Dex. But yet the niggas went down irregardless 'cause they're black and 'cause the court said they acted *in concert.*

But my question for you is: *Why Dexter go running into that building when he heard gunshots?* It just goes to show how ignorant he was. You run *away* when you hear gunshots. It's just common sense. Nigga's got to know that. It's like that guy Darwin's theory. Survival of the fittest. You know what I'm saying? It's like Dex wasn't right in the head, like he wasn't meant to live. Like he was too good in a way. Too good to survive in a fucked up world.

You know what I'm saying?

I mean, why'd he do that? Why'd he run into that building? It don't make no sense. Why he didn't just let me be?

No, Kevin's all right. Or Africa, whatever—I still call him Kevin. He shot himself in the foot, but he's going to be fine. The doctors say he'll be out of the hospital tomorrow. He'll just be limping around some. That's all.

Who, me?

Eddy. I'm Eddy.

Yeah. Fast Eddy.

Actually, I have no idea why people call me *Fast Eddy.* Maybe just because it sounds right. I think there was a Fast Eddy who played basketball back in the day, but I don't know, and, to be truthful, I don't care. I think it's kind of stupid, personally. I don't call myself it.

Yeah, I suppose I got a couple of minutes. But then I've got to head back to work. I took an extra half hour on Monday, and my new supervisor's going to get pissed off if I do it twice in one week. He's not so bad though—I mean, for a supervisor.

Right now?

Well, *right now* I work over on Forty Ninth and Sixth. Doing the mailroom thing. It's not brain work, you know, just lots of lifting and sorting, that kind of stuff. But I'm meeting people, making contacts. They treat me pretty good, the folks in the building. I walk into their office, I get lots of chit chat. The salesmen want to talk Knicks. Truthfully, I don't give a rat's ass about basketball, but I hear them out, you know, just listen and smile, because that's how the game is played. Eventually, I've got my eye on sales. If not with the company I'm with now, then somewhere else. That's the master plan. That's down the road, but meanwhile I'm getting paid pretty good. It's going to happen for me.

What?

How do the *women* treat me? You mean, like, the secretaries? Or do you mean the female execs? The only reason I'm asking is because it's two different answers.

Well, the secretaries are about half and half. Half treat me all right, but half don't bother with me. It's nothing personal, the half that don't bother with me; or if it *is* personal, I don't take it that way. It's just a class thing. Like they get dumped on all day, so they turn around and dump on the guys from the mailroom. Maybe it's not even half of them that are like that. Maybe it's even less.

Now the female execs, that's another story. With them, it's the black thing. You know . . . like how well-off white women act with black men. They look me straight in the eyes, they touch me a lot, put their hands on my arm when they talk to me. It's as if they're trying to say: *I'm on your side. I feel your pain. I support your struggle.* The assumption being that since I'm black, I must be struggling against something. The thing about well-off white women with black men is that they're always out to show how they're not afraid of us. It's kind of silly, but I don't blame them. They don't mean nothing bad by it. They're just trying too hard. In a way, it's like that's *their* struggle. Me, personally? I don't got no struggle. Me, personally, I like to be and let be.

Tell me again why you're taping this?

All right, but I thought it was Kevin you were interested in. . . .

That's kind of a strange question. I mean, if you don't get what makes him interesting, why have you spent so much time talking to him? He's interesting to me because he's my friend. I've known Kevin since junior high. But even if we didn't have the history, he'd be interesting—at least in my opinion. For one thing, he's smart. Real smart. It don't always come across that way, how smart Kevin is. I mean, he can go off in different directions with what he says. Honestly, I don't know how much of it he believes himself. But I'll tell you one thing for sure. If you compare him with Jerome, brain-wise, it's no contest. As far as I'm concerned, Jerome's nothing but a damn fool.

Take it from me.

Yeah, Jerome dragged me to one of those *Free Mumia* rallies once. Never again though. First off, the brother did the crime. Mumia, I mean. I wasn't sure at first, but I heard so much double talk about *Oppression* and *Injustice* that by the end I knew he did it. That's always how you can tell. When folks talk about stuff that has nothing to do with what they're supposed to be talking about, it means they've got no case. It wasn't just the speakers either. Half the folks there didn't give a rat's ass about Mumia Abu Jamal. He was just their excuse to raise a ruckus. They had their own angles to work. Man, I ain't never been handed so much useless paper. Communist Party. Socialist Workers' Party. Green Party. Women's Lib. Indian Rights. It was like that on stage too. There was a biker-looking chick giving a speech about a queer kid who got beat to death in Kansas. Or Colorado, some place like that. Then she talked about Mumia for a couple of minutes. Then she talked about date rape for a couple more minutes. She kept shouting how, *It's all the same thing! It's all the same thing! It's all the same thing!* That's about when I got handed a piece of paper from NAMBLA. You know what that is? That's grown men who fuck little boys—pardon the cuss word. I mean, *child molesters!* But they had their papers going around with the rest.

It was a damn circus is what it was.

But Jerome, he just eats that stuff up. He even hopped up onto the stage and talked near the end. He got introduced as a *Doctor of Philosophy*—which is a damn lie. He ain't going to earn no doctor's degree if he stays in school till he's a hundred years old. But he stepped up to that microphone, and he worked the crowd; he even got them to chant. The joke of it was, it wasn't even his Mumia chant that got them going. No, what got them going was:

The people . . . united . . .

Can never be defeated!

Except, if you ask me, the *people* aren't never going to get behind nothing the folks at that rally wanted. The only thing the people *might* get behind is dropping a great big net over that crowd and dumping them in the Hudson River. Anyway, after an entire afternoon of listening to them, that's what *I* could've got behind.

I mean, I don't want to beat the thing to death, but you got one speaker after another climbing up onto that stage, talking about *people of color.* Talking about how *people of color* got to unite. You want to know the truth? I hate that! You know what *people of color* is? That's just a bunch of Dominicans and Puerto Ricans and Arabs and Asians trying to pretend that their histories are just like black folks' history. Kevin's actually the one who pointed that out to me—how *people of color* is a bunch of crap. I mean, I can see why *they'd* want to pretend that; it gives them, you know, an edge. You know what I'm saying? Like their ancestors got wronged just as bad as ours, so now it's their turn to get paid. What gets me is why black folks would stand around and listen to them talking about *people of color* and don't say nothing against it.

So, yeah, Jerome's full of crap. Kevin's got more brains in his pinky finger than Jerome's got in his entire skull. Did he ever show you the cube trick? Man, I ain't never seen nothing like it. You can mess up that cube for an hour, set it up so none of the colors are even close, and then hand it back to him. He stares at it for about ten seconds, and then it's like *boom, boom, boom,* and he's done. I've seen him do it in less than two minutes. Six sides, perfect, like it was nothing. I sat with that damn cube for a week, and the best I could do was one side.

But it ain't just the cube. It's how he gets things. True, he don't make good grades—like I said, I've known Kevin since seventh grade, and he didn't never make good grades. But he *gets it,* whatever it is. It don't matter if it's social studies or if it's math or poems or what have you. He gets it. He tutored me in statistics senior year of high school; ain't no way I would've gotten through that subject if he didn't spend hours after class doing it with me. But the thing is, I wound up with a higher grade than Kevin did. Not because I knew statistics better, but because he didn't give a rat's ass about making a good grade. He squeaked by with like a C-minus, whereas I got a B.

It's a damn waste is what it is, the fact that Kevin never made good grades. The fact that he never tried for college. I mean, the brother should've wound up an engineer or something. He had it in him. Ain't nothing Kevin couldn't have done if he'd had a mind to do it.

Truthfully, it makes me kind of sad just to talk about it. It's like a tragedy, except smaller—how Kevin's life came out. I mean, it's not like Rwanda. Now that's a *tragedy*. You know what I'm saying? But it *is* sad how Kevin's life came out. Well, in my opinion, it's sad. Maybe not for him. . . . Actually, I think he's pretty happy. If you told him it was tragic how his life came out, Kevin would probably look at you like you was crazy. But sometimes I catch sight of him on the street corner, you know, doing what he does, and I get a kind of sick feeling in my guts. You know? It's like he's down on the corner passing dime bags; whereas he should be up at Columbia passing engineering tests.

Now don't get me wrong. I know lots of brothers doing lots worse things than Kevin. Half the brothers I know are like *looking* to do time. I mean that, truthfully: I'm talking brothers who *want* to take a stretch. You know, nothing too hard. Maybe like 90 days for weapons. Just enough to brag about it at barbecues, just enough to talk up the ladies. It's like brothers think that's what makes them black; I mean *authentic* black. Original Gangster—that's the mentality. You know what I'm talking about?

What's worse is the ladies gobble it up. You go to a barbecue down in East New York, who do you think the ladies crowd around? The brother working his butt off for a job promotion? Or the brother who's got to step inside to phone his parole officer? I seen it a hundred times. Some thug-ass wannabe talking trash, surrounded by ladies, and meanwhile five brothers who ain't never been locked down are off sitting by themselves, like they're ashamed. Plus, it's like a vicious circle—because the younger generation, they see what it takes to get next to ladies, so now they're busy scheming how they're going to get their own reps. And on and on and on.

If you look at it like that, the vicious circle I mean, it almost *is* a tragedy. It almost *is* Rwanda.

You know?

Dorinda's like that. Caramel too. Always looking for the thug. It's a damn shame too, at least with Dorinda, because she's got a decent heart. Keisha used to be that way too, you know, thugging it up, but then she got it in her head she was going to get with Kevin permanent—which has about as much chance of happening as me getting with Mariah Carey. Kevin don't even mess with her no more, Keisha I mean, because he don't want to encourage her. It breaks your heart to watch the two of them together. How she goes mental the second he walks in the room. How he spends nights dodging her like she's infected with something.

Except what she's infected with is him. She's got it bad.

Who, me?

I guess I'd go with Dorinda if she'd have me. But she won't, not as long as I'm doing the nine-to-five thing. And if I've got to be a thug to go with Dorinda, then I'd rather be alone. Besides, that's another way brothers mess up. They get caught up being with someone before they're ready to settle down—I mean, in terms of money, in terms of feelings, in terms of life. Right now, I look at myself in the mirror, and I know I ain't ready. I'm like a *work in progress*. Ain't nothing to be ashamed of, the fact that you still got more growing up to do. The shameful thing is when you front.

That's just my opinion.

I *am* partial to Dorinda though. I've been with her once too, almost twice, so it ain't like a trophy situation. The thing about Dorinda is you can talk to her. Tell her what your dreams are, tell her how long you figure it's going to take. You know what I'm talking about? Plus, it's not like she just listens neither. She makes comments. She tells you when you're full of crap. Like I was telling her once about how I came up with a suggestion for the Suggestion Box in the mailroom . . . how I wrote it out a couple of times, how I typed it up nice and neat, how I folded up the paper real tight so no one else could read it, how I dropped it in the box when no one was watching, how I figured the old supervisor was going to read it and right off make me his assistant. She just started to laugh. She said, first of all, the supervisor wasn't going to read it—no one was. Said, second of all, even if the supervisor did read it, he was going to feel like I was just being uppity. Said, third of all, even if he did read it, and even if he thought it was a good idea, he was only going to take credit for it himself and then probably fire my suggestion-writing ass to cover himself.

What?

I think she was right in the first place; no one ever read it.

But the point is, she didn't just nod at what I was saying—like how ladies tend to do. I guess she figured I wasn't a thug, so she knew she could never get serious with me. Maybe if I was a thug, she would've just nodded. But it was kind of a friendship thing for her. The sex, I mean. The entire night was like friendship. Lots of laughing and talking. The sex was just kind of the reason for the rest of the night. What I mean is it was the *reason,* but it wasn't the main thing. Just the thing that brought us together.

So, yeah, Dorinda's the one I'd go with. But it ain't going to happen, and that's that. There's worse things in life than not getting with who you want to get with. You know what I'm saying?

Anyway, I should be going. . . .

No, I don't know no more than what I already said. Only that Kevin shot himself in the foot. I wasn't there; I don't know how it happened. Herc's real pissed at me for not riding with them. They're all pissed at me—Herc, Jerome, Raheem, Keisha, Caramel. Even Kevin was down on me when I said I wasn't riding. But then he phoned me from the hospital last night and said I could make it up to him by finding you and letting you know what happened. I could hear he was still a little pissed though. But, truthfully, I don't care. It was pointless anyway. Nothing happened. I don't know how much Kevin told you about it; the entire thing was because Herc heard talk about a brother from the Bronx. I suppose he owed Herc money too; Herc wouldn't bother with the Bronx unless there was money involved; I just don't think it was *that* much. Mainly, I think, it was Herc's rep. It don't matter, whatever it was, because last night the two of them got together and worked it out. They were just standing around, Herc's people and the Bronx people, just smiling and mingling, when Kevin shot himself in the foot. Knowing him, he was probably just being curious. Probably wanting to figure out how the thing worked—on the inside, I mean. Keisha said no one was near him when it went off. Said the rest of them was trying hard not to laugh while they was dropping him off at the emergency room.

So, like I said, they're all pissed at me now. Herc especially. He's making it into a big old deal, the fact that I didn't ride with them. Like it's, you know, *symbolic*. You know what I'm saying? Like it proves something about me he's been suspecting all along.

You want to know why I didn't go?

I'll say it straight out: I was scared.

I ain't ashamed of it neither. Why should I lay it down for Herc? And not even for Herc, when you stop and think about it—for Herc's *rep!* What's the brother ever done for me? I ain't never asked him for nothing. I think, *once,* I borrowed a hundred dollars from him. But that was years ago, and he got back every damn penny inside a couple of weeks. I don't like owing nothing to nobody. I know brothers always borrowing from A to pay off B—which, you know, I could almost understand. It happens. I don't condemn them for it because brothers get down on their luck. The brother I condemn is the one who's borrowing left and right, and meanwhile he's out styling with gold chains. That's all I'm saying.

I mean, what's that about? It don't compute.

Me, personally?

No, I ain't like that. First off, I don't wear no chains. Second off, I don't believe in debt. If I don't got the dough, I don't buy the goods. That's the rule I live by. I got credit card companies mailing me their stuff every week. Offering me lines of five thousand dollars. But I just tear up the envelopes. I don't even read them. Half the time, I don't even open them. I just rip them in half and file them in the trash can next to the mailbox.

So what if Herc think I'm a Tom? I mean, that's Herc's opinion. That, plus a dollar-and-a-half buys you a subway token. I ain't living my life to please no thug ass wannabe. No, I take that back. He ain't no wannabe. Herc's a thug. The genuine article. I'll give him that. He's hardcore.

But that don't make his opinion worth no more than mine.

He says I'm Tommin' around. . . . I say I'm just being me.

So who's right, and who's wrong?

I ain't saying no more on the subject.

But I'll let you in on a little secret. It ain't even a secret, actually. It's more like a suspicion. I think Herc's the one who whacked Dexter—you know, Kevin's brother. Kevin told me he talked to you about Dexter. Now if you want to know what *I* think happened, there it is. I think Herc whacked Dexter. Plus, I think he did it on purpose. I think he was pissed that Dexter followed the two of them to Brooklyn that night, and I think Herc blew him away.

No, I don't got no evidence. It's just how Herc talks about it. Like he always skips over that part of the story.

Actually, I came straight out once and asked him if he whacked Dexter. The two of us was alone, in the back room of a club. The music was pumping. Both of us was a little tight. Loose and tight at the same time. You know what I mean? And the thing is, he didn't deny it. I asked him if he whacked Dexter, and he didn't deny it. He just kind of smiled at me—like I should've known not to ask him that question. I mean, if it ain't the truth, I think he would've denied it. I know I would've denied it if it wasn't the truth. But, the thing was, it didn't even bother him—the fact that I asked. It didn't even surprise him. He just kind of smiled at me and didn't answer.

The more I think about it, the more sure I am: Herc whacked Dexter. . . .

Say, what time is it?

Damn, I got to get back to work!

Kevin'll be here next week, like usual. Like I said, he ain't hurt too bad.

WELL, GO ON: I SEE YOU'RE SMILING.

Get it out of your system.

It *is* humorous, a nigga shooting his own self in the foot. Ain't nothing you can say going to make me feel more dumb stupid than I already feel. I mean, that kind of shit only happens in cartoons. Coyote motherfucker. You know what I'm saying? So if you want to laugh, I don't mind.

I'm going to just lean the crutches against the chair, okay?

No, I can do it myself.

The doctor said four to six weeks. But I'm getting used to them already.

I guess Eddy already told you what happened up in the Bronx. Besides the foot shooting, I mean. It was like I predicted. Niggas got together and worked it out. Ain't nothing niggas can't work out if they got a mind to. *Mentality,* that's the key. If it wasn't for me getting dumb stupid with the damn Glock, we could've had like a cookout or something.

By the way, Eddy feels real bad about how he bailed. Looking back, I can kind of understand where he was coming from, in a way. Eddy's a lot like me; we both kind of pacifistic. But there comes a point when you got to go to war, when you got to do what you got to do. I was scared too, yo, but yet I did what I had to do. I got Herc's back. Meanwhile, now Herc's all the time hatin' on Eddy, saying how he's an Uncle Tom. I don't think he is, personally. But I *did* lose respect for him. No other way to say it. It's like as if he was tested, and he failed. Like as if he failed at being a man. I love Eddy to death, but, for real, it's like as if he failed at being a man.

You know what I'm saying?

Meanwhile, I had lots of time to think. You know? I mean, like, *think.* That night I spent in the hospital, I did some serious cogitating. The conclusion I came to is that what we're doing right now, you and me, it's like maybe the most important thing I've ever done. Getting the truth out. Making black folks hold their heads up proud. It's like that's what I was born for. You know what I'm saying? It's the reason God put me on the planet.

Yo, check it out.

It's like I was lying in that hospital bed, and all of a sudden I realized that my whole entire life was preparing me for this project. Everything I learned. Everything I felt. It was just getting me ready to educate my people about who they are and where they came from. Black folks got to know that they the dominant race, that whatever white folks got is stole from them. Same with chinks. It's all stole from black folks, like I said in the beginning. The inventions. The writings. The pictures. But the worst thing that got stole was black folks' *self-esteem.* That's the worst thing you can steal from a people. Make them feel all worthless. Make them feel like they ain't did nothing.

That's what got stole from us, self-esteem.

So the question is, how do we get it back? That's what I was wondering to myself in that hospital room. How do black folks get back the self-esteem that was took from them by white folks?

The answer came to me like *that.*

It's the younger generation. The younger generation got to teach the elders to respect their selves.

That's the main reason I called my old man from the hospital. I'm riding out to Queens to have lunch with him tomorrow. Not for my sake. For his. I realized I got to teach him to respect his self. 'Cause my old man *is* an Uncle Tom. He don't mean to be, but the white man stole his self-esteem, and he don't even know it. It's on me to raise him up. To raise his awareness. His self-consciousness. You know what I'm saying? He's been dragged down, and I got to raise him back up.

But not just him. Not even just black folks. It's on the younger generation to raise up *all* people. That's what came to me when I was lying in the hospital. Liberation is what I'm talking about. Liberation for *all* people, worldwide. Black. White. Chinks. Spics. It don't matter. It's on the younger generation to liberate the minds of the elders.

'Cause when you get down to it, yo, it's the mind that keeps people in chains. It ain't physical chains no more. It's mental. You know what I'm saying? It's *mentality* that keeps people in chains.

Her?

No, the bitch didn't call. She will, sooner or later. The reason I'm so sure is it's like the saying goes: "Once you go black, you never go back!" But the thing about Liang is—if she don't call, fuck her! It's like as if that night in the hospital got me squared away. Not just my foot, neither. My brain too. I thought Liang was one of the few. But it turned out she was one of the many. Hey, I should've known that in the first place 'cause there's like about ten billion chinks.

What I'm saying is Liang's not a real person. I mean, naturally, she's real. I didn't make her up. But she's not *real.* She don't give it up like a real person. I'm not talking her pussy so much as her soul. You know? Another couple of weeks, and for sure I'd have got her sucking and fucking. But I still wouldn't have got her soul. I still wouldn't have got *her.* It ain't the same thing, fucking Liang's pussy and fucking Liang. It's like a concept. The two of them are related. But yet they're not the same thing. It's hard to get across what I mean. It's deep.

That's what it'll do to you, lying awake all night in a hospital bed, staring at the bullet the doctors just yanked out your body. I stared at it practically the whole entire night. It was sitting in a plastic cup on the table next to my bed. Every so often, I picked it out of the cup and squeezed it in my fist. I squeezed it real tight till it got warm, like the same temperature as my body. Which is where it was for an hour. It makes you think.

You want to see it? The bullet?
Yeah, I got it in my back pocket.
Go on, take it!
See how the nose is squished in? That's where it hit my foot bone. It almost don't even look like a bullet no more. Like a crushed-up can is more like it. Except littler. The doctors cleaned the blood off before they gave it to me. Actually, I think it would've been kind of dope if it still had my blood on it. Kind of like gruesome.
Damn straight I'm going to keep it!
Putting it on a chain next week.
Now the very fact you even got to ask means you still don't know nothing about black people. You want to know the reason I'm putting it on a necklace? I spell that *p-u-s-s-y*. Females love shit like that. *Love it, love it, can't get enough of it!* Yo, that bullet's like a free ticket to Chickenhead City.
Gotta suck that dick up, till ya hiccup!
You *do* know what I'm talking 'bout, don't you?
Heh, heh, I thought so!
Yo sisters, it's your birthday!
It's your birthday!
It's your birthday!
What?
Well, I guess it's 'cause I looked death square in the eye. It's like I learned to appreciate life. When you appreciate life, yo, sometimes you just feel like singing. You know?
Dorinda, it's your birthday!
It's your birthday!
It's your birthday!
So that's the reason I'm putting the bullet on a chain. It's an example of what I call *forward thinking*. That's the key. You always got to be thinking forward. You got to deal with what's going on today, no doubt, but also you got to keep your eyes on the prize.
You know what I'm saying?
Actually, when I think back on being shot, you know what kind of touched me in the whole thing? It's how Herc

came by to pick me up the next morning. He showed up at the hospital in a Benz! He could've drove over in a Civic or something, but he rolled up in a shiny black Benz. The chink nurse that wheeled me to the door, you should've seen the look on her face. Like she couldn't believe a black man would be driving a Benz—which is how most chinks think. Liang, for sure, thinks like that. She would've never thought Herc would do something so thoughtful. I mean, he must've dropped a couple of Franklins for that Benz, and he only needed it for like an hour or so. When he popped open that shiny black door, and he cranked forward that leather seat for me to slide in the back—yo, I was *feeling* him. You know? I felt like the king of the motherfucking world. He drove me all the way home like that, like he was the chauffeur, and I was king of the motherfucking world.

It was like that flick, *Driving Miss Daisy*—except for the fact that I ain't no old white cunt. Plus, Herc ain't no house nigga like the brother in the movie. Actually, when you think about it, it ain't like that flick at all. But what I'm saying is Herc went the extra mile to make me feel good. It was thoughtful of him. That's all I'm saying.

What?

Do I love Herc? Now that's a fool question to ask.

Hey, I got nothing *but* love for him, baby!

I ain't ashamed to say it neither. 'Cause it ain't no faggy thing, love. Lots of niggas I know, they be all caught up in their own macho shit—like *I can't love no males since I'm into pussy.* But me, I think love comes in lots of different ways. Looking back over my life, to be truthful, I think I probably loved more brothers than sisters. And that don't make me no faggot. So, yeah, damn straight I love Herc. I love Eddy too. Hey, I even love Jerome sometimes—like when he forgets about Mumia for ten minutes, and he's just plain old Jerome. Keisha too, though with Keisha I got to be careful how I show it.

I love all of 'em . . . and I let 'em know it too. Not in so many words, but I let 'em know.

How?

Well, take an example. Sometimes me and Herc'll be walking down a dark street late at night, no one else around, and I'll just kind of nudge him with my shoulder. Like we accidental bumped shoulders, except it's not by accident, and both of us know it. It's like as if to say: *Hey, I'm feeling you, bro.* Except without words.

So, yeah, love.

I'm into it.

If you look at things from a spiritual point of view, when all's said and done, what else is there besides love? That's what separates us from the animals. You know what I'm saying? It's what makes us human beings.

Yo, that's the most spiritual thing a white boy ever said: *All you need is love.* I'll give credit where credit is due. It's one of the few white songs I can bear to listen to. *All you need is love.*

No diggity—I dig it.

But the thing of it is, you don't got to be *in love* with somebody to love somebody. For a time, I thought I was *in love* with Liang. But I never actually *loved* her. You know what I'm saying? When I was with her, I felt like I was mad crazy in love. But I was never actually *feeling* her. It's like, you know how sometimes you're walking up a flight of stairs, and you think there's one more step at the top, except it ain't there, and then you step down on nothing. It rattles up your insides. Well, that's like how it was when I was with Liang. Like I was always taking that step that wasn't there. Like I kept stepping up, but I wasn't coming down on nothing. I wasn't getting nothing back is what I'm saying.

That's what taking a bullet does to you. You know? It puts things into perspective. Everything. Everyone. It's like it clears out your brain and makes you *prioritize.*

Actually, I got another example. You know who I started feeling after I got shot?

Dorinda.

That's one of Keisha's girls. The afternoon I came home from the hospital, she'd already gone and left a message on my machine. Just to check in, find out how I was doing. The reason that touched me is I ain't never even done her. I done just about all of Keisha's girls, but I ain't never done Dorinda. Never felt a reason to 'cause she's been stuck more times than a twelve foot jumper. Plus, baby's got a little *too much* back. You know what I'm saying? But that message she left on the machine, it touched me. It told me something about her as a human being, the fact that she called to find out did I need stuff. Like groceries. She left a long message about how I needed to drink a lot of juice till the bone heals up. She knows what she's talking 'bout too 'cause a couple of her men got shot up before. I guess that's the reason she called. She knows what it's like.

I called her back and told her I didn't need nothing, but she swung by that afternoon irregardless. When she showed up, she was toting a pair of big old brown bags that was full of shit, you know, sandwiches and o.j. Plus, shit like peroxide and bandages—which actually I did need 'cause the doc told me to change the dressing every so often. Well, she's unloading the shit onto the kitchen table until she comes to the second bag, and then she reaches in and hauls out a six of 45's. I mean, that really got to me.

Then I said, "Now how'd you know? Eddy put you up to it?"

She just kind of smiles. "You always remind me of Billy D."

"You crazy, woman! I don't look nothing like no Billy D.!"

"You got a smooth way about you. That's what I'm saying."

Then I just kind of laughed, like *heh, heh.* You know, like not *hah, hah.* More like a laugh that means we both know where the conversation's going. That kind of laugh. Except of course it ain't going there, the conversation I mean, not right at that moment, 'cause I lost a lot of blood the night before, and I got, you know, bandages and dressings on my foot. But that *heh, heh*—that's like a note, like an I.O.U. It's like a contract between the two of us, me and Dorinda, like as if to say: *Not now, not yet, but it's going to be our time soon enough.*

When you stop and think about it, it's almost like black folks got a kind of *heh, heh* thing going with white folks. Like black folks and white folks both know, sooner or later, black folks going to wind up on top. 'Cause that's the natural way of things. I don't mean to get all intellectual about it. But the thing is, if you look at history, in a way, it's like a game of hoops. White folks got out on a run in the first half, true that, knocked down a mess of three-pointers, like white boys sometimes do, but if you take a look at both sides, if you take a *close up* look, if you look at the thing *realistic* is what I mean, you just know, as the game goes on, black folks going to come back. White folks can't run with black folks. Can't. That's a proven fact. When it's the final whistle, you watch and see who's on top.

Huh?

No, it don't have to be like that. It ain't about payback. Well, maybe a little, in the beginning. But once black folks get back on top, black folks *and* white folks going to be better off than ever. 'Cause things won't be so fucked up. Chinks and spics too. The world's going to be a better place. Ain't going to be no more wars 'cause niggas sit down and work that shit out—like what happened with Herc and the Bronx. Won't be no more nuclear bombs falling the second some country gets pissed off. Won't even be no more countries, probably. Just like *brotherhood.* You know what I'm saying? Brothers be running things, so it's brotherhood, you know, overseeing shit, so ain't going to be no more wars. That's what I predict.

As it was in the beginning, so shall it be in the end.
That's from the Koran. You could look it up.

173

Allah, he was down with that kind of shit. Future predictions. The so-called Armaggedon. The end of the world is what I'm talking about. It's all down in black and white, in the Koran. When you stop to think about it, God was the Original Gangsta. He made the world just so he could smoke it. That's the gangsta mentality right there in a nutshell. 'Cause the gangsta knows ain't nothing permanent. Not even God is permanent.

The whole idea of "permanent" is actually a white thing. The reason why is 'cause the white man, he's scared of dying. Death . . . that scares the shit out of the white man. That's his weakness. Why do you think he spends so much time trying to figure out science? It's 'cause the white man's scared of dying. He's always looking for a cure. That why he always gives it up for the Jews. He figures Jew doctors got the best chance to figure out a cure. Or maybe, if a Jew doctor can't figure out a cure, maybe the white man can hire a Jew lawyer to work out a deal for him. Except Allah don't got no time for no beanie-wearing Jew lawyer. Or Jew doctor neither. It ain't no use.

No Jew's going to weasel the white man out of death.

The ironical thing is that if anyone was ever going to figure out a cure for death, it would've for sure been the black man. So, in a way, if the white man hadn't stolen science from the black man, the white man might not be so scared of dying today. 'Cause it's for sure the black man would've shared the cure; that's his nature. That's the reason he couldn't fight back against the white man. He was used to folks just being folks. Being good is what I mean. He wasn't prepared for the evil of the white man. He saw them ugly pale things dragging themselves through the jungle, trying to explore, and he took pity on 'em. That was his fatal mistake, being innocent. It just never dawned on him that the white man would stab him in the back.

So, yeah, the black man probably could've figured out a cure for death. But that ain't what he's about. He looks at death as part of the circle. You know what I'm saying. Birth. Death. And on and on, right into et cetera.

That's part of the secret wisdom that lives inside every black man. It was handed down, generation to generation, from his ancestors—yo, I'm talking way back to the Nubians. Except it was handed down *without words*. That's the kick of it. It ain't the kind of wisdom you got to read up on in books. It's in the heart. You know what I'm saying? If you black, you born with it. The Wisdom of the Nubians is what it's called.

Me, personally, I just call it *soul*.

You know what I'm saying?

I'll bet you didn't know the Nubians could levitate, did you?

What?

Yeah, that's right. I thought I did. I lose track sometimes—

Say what?

Yo!

You run out of tape or something? 'Cause I can easy set you up—

Yo, man, that's cold. That's stone cold.

That's like . . . *yo!*

Is it 'cause I insulted you just now—I mean, with what I said about the white man? I didn't mean it to sound like that. It's just that I thought we'd got to a point where I didn't have to front. I mean, the truth ain't always pretty. That's a fact of life. But if I said something, all right, my bad. . . .

What?

Yo, if it ain't that, then what's the reason?

All right, but how do you *know* we done?

How do you know I ain't got lots more shit to tell? Don't you want to find out what happens with my old man tomorrow? *Yo*, I ain't told you but a fraction of what I got on my mind.

What?

All right. All right.

Whatever.

Ain't no *thang.* You know what I'm saying?

Then we leave it like this: We done *for now.*

What you thanking me for? I didn't do none of this for you. I did it to get the truth out. That's always been the reason. Or else why would I waste my time not getting paid?

If we done, we done.

A salaam aleichem.

Peace. One love. We out.